Stepping Out

Clare ... educated at Felixsto... nd. Her first two chil... the family moved to ... nglish literature and ... born. She studied p... Hong Kong and then l... ng University for eight years.

Currently she lectures in psychology at Macquarie University and practises as a family therapist. She lives in Sydney with her second husband and has children in Australia, Britain, Canada and Hong Kong.

Dr Clare Harding

Stepping Out

Surviving a Stepfamily.

PAN

First published 1994 by Pan Macmillan Children's Books

a division of Pan Macmillan Publishers Limited
Cavaye Place London SW10 9PG
and Basingstoke

Associated companies throughout the world

ISBN 0–330–33339–9

1 3 5 7 9 8 6 4 2

A CIP catalogue record for this book is available from
the British Library

Phototypeset by Intype, London
Printed by Cox & Wyman Ltd, Reading, Berkshire

Acknowledgements

I am grateful to Erica De'Ath for getting me en route to publication and to my editor, Isabel Barratt, whose warmth, enthusiasm and expertise made working on the book a rewarding experience.

Many thanks to Marion Orchison, who read the manuscript in serial form with her friends at school and who saved me from many pitfalls. Also thanks to Penelope Lamaro, Natalie Barrett, Tracie Ainsworth, Gemma Dolan, and Sabrina Lynch, for their comments and encouragement and, of course, to all the teenagers who share their doubts, fears and hopes with me as a family therapist.

To my children, Caroline, Rosalind, Frances and Dickon, for the richness and pleasure they add to my life.

Also for Stephen, who introduced me to stepfamilies.

Dear Donna

We had a great time in the Solomon Islands. You wouldn't believe how warm the water is. I learned to spear fish with a harpoon. It's really hard because the fish are never where you think they are, so you have to aim off. But I got the hang of it in the end and I'm sending you this photo of me holding this enormous fish I caught all by myself. Actually, Dad helped me with the last bit. I hate their teeth. We ate it. Dad put his in lemon and left it in the sun and then ate it. Yuk! The rest of us cooked ours. Sometimes the sharks bit the tails off the fish while we were reeling them in.

I got a bit bored on the boat sometimes, but the islands were great. Everyone was really friendly, especially the girls. They wore grass skirts and nothing on top so there was nothing left to the imagination!!! Lots of them spoke English because of the mission schools. I'm going to send them some make-up, Dad says he'll help me pay for it. He got really sick on the boat. We sailed for twenty-four hours to one island.

The weather was gross, lots of rain and wind. Dad had his mattress on the deck and just lay there letting the water wash over him each time the boat rolled. It was quite warm but he looked awful. His eyes sort of sunk in and his hair went all stringy. He chucked up a lot too. Another old man tried to go inside and cut his head on a nail. There was blood everywhere and he made a terrible fuss. He had an upset tummy and went

1

over the side of the boat. Yuk. He was horrible anyway, so I didn't feel that sorry for him. He was always swearing at me when Dad wasn't around and pretending to be nice to me when he was. I didn't get sick at all because Peter, who was the captain, gave me some anti-seasick pills.

When we got to the island the sun came out and it was really hot. We went in a truck for ages and then we all split up and went to lots of different places. We walked for miles and I was so thirsty I could have died. Then some of the men climbed the coconut trees and knocked down some coconuts. You have to be careful not to stand too near, they are deadly. We cut the tops off and inside was this lovely cool watery milk. I've never tasted anything so good. Then they split the nuts open and there was this spongy stuff inside which tasted a bit of coconut. That night we slept in some huts on mats. The village people came to give us a concert but I was so tired I fell asleep. Dad says they sang and danced for about three hours and I missed it all.

It felt funny getting home again and being able to eat pizzas and chips. I don't think I ever want to eat rice or fish again. The cats were really pleased to see us. Dill was very thin and mournful looking, but Razoo was just the same as ever. He rolled over and purred and purred. Everyone says I look great because my sun-bleached hair is weird with my brown eyes. Matthew rang as soon as we got home. He said he really, really missed me. I went over to his place for the day and we talked and talked in his bedroom. He's painted it grey with one black wall and he's got motor-bike posters all over it. Some of them are terrific. He's mad about Wayne Gardner.

His Mum kept coming in to ask did we want coffee or anything to eat and to get him to do things for her. She's so funny when she tries to be tactful like that. I like her. I don't know how I lasted in the Solomons without Matthew, he makes me laugh so much. He's personality plus and what a body!!!!! He says he didn't even see Melissa as she was up in Queensland with her parents. I'd have killed her if she'd got her claws into him.

Dad got malaria three days after we got home. He is very unlucky. In the end I had to ring Gran because he was shivering so much and couldn't drive to the doctor. I tried to get him to eat something but he wouldn't even eat his favourite poppy-seed rolls. Sometimes I worry about him. I went off to Mum's for the week so Dad could have some peace while Gran looked after him. I hated not being there with Gran because she's special, but it was about time I saw Mum and I know she misses me when I go on trips. She was pleased to see me I think. She'd been to Hobart and had a good time. I don't think she enjoyed her Christmas though. It's so difficult deciding whether to spend it with Mum or Dad, sometimes I wish they were still together. Life would be much easier. I wonder whether parents think of their kids when they decide to divorce, it's not very fair on us when we don't have a say in it. And now *you* aren't even here for me to talk to, so I'm feeling a bit fed up. It's boring without you. How long do you think you'll have to stay in Hong Kong? What's your new school like? What year did you go into in the end? And what are the kids like, are there lots of Chinese? You are so lucky. David says he'll never forget you and he'll write every week. Bet he doesn't.

3

School starts the day after tomorrow. I hope we don't have Sharky for maths, if we do I'm going to ask to change classes, he really hates me I know. Send me some Chinese jokes I can play on him. The netball team isn't going to be any good without you and I'll have to find a new partner in gym.

Yours feeling fed up,
Brook

Feb 22nd

Dear Donna

Whew! Back at school a whole three weeks. I'm in the top group for Maths, English and Social Studies which means no Sharky. Isn't that ace! I've got netball again for sport. Mum said I should try something else, but I didn't want to. I think I'll do pretty well in the swimming so that should keep her happy. Melissa is full of this guy she met in Queensland, eighteen and mega sexy according to her. She went to the movies with Michael on Friday night. She's a real moll. You should see the letters she gets from this Queensland guy who she says is going to come down to see her for Easter, and then she goes with Michael. He doesn't know about Queensland. I feel sorry for him, he's a sweet guy but too naive for Melissa. He'll get hurt. David is still miserable without you, but there is a new spooner called Rachel who fancies him. I'll keep you posted. What's the talent like in Hong Kong?

We went surfing yesterday at Palm Beach. Matt got a new board for Christmas, an Emerald square tail. It's five foot ten. I had a few gos on it but it takes some getting used to after my old tri-fin. You should see me hang ten or do a tube, it's unreal. Matthew thinks I'm different from other girls because I love surfing and sailing and will try anything. He smothered my back and legs with sun-tan oil. Just feeling his hands stroking my back made me feel all shivery. He's got some new

5

board shorts, black and white, and he looks real cute in them. I could eat him.

Bren and Emma and David came with us and we asked Rachel because she doesn't know many people round here. She sails too, so next week we're going to the Pittwater side. Dad says he can fix for us to borrow a couple of sailboards. He's been grumbling because he never sees me at the weekend, he picks me up from Mum's on Saturday nights and then I spend all Sunday with Matthew and the others. He doesn't seem to realize that I need to be with my friends, and anyway I've just spent a whole month in the Solomons with him.

Actually I'm getting a bit fed up of spending half the week with Mum and half with Dad. I feel as if I'm always camping. I never have half the clothes I want in the right place and if I leave one of my school books at Mum's then I have to go without it until I go back there on Tuesday afternoon. It would be much easier if I could just go round and pick things up but they get so cranky when I do that. They ring each other and it always ends in an argument with Dad yelling and Mum crying, and then I feel terrible because it's my fault.

Matthew says they should only ring when I'm not there. I think that's a good idea, I'll see what Dad thinks. At least Mum has stopped asking me about Dad and what he's doing and what I did at his place. It's none of her business anyway, after all, they were the ones who split. It makes me angry with her because I'm pulled both ways. I don't think she really likes me having a good time at Dad's, so it's better not to talk about it. If I get home before she gets back from school then I have time to veg out for a bit and watch a video and then I feel better.

Best of all is when Mum and I eat out on Tuesdays, that's fun. Last week I made dinner, spaghetti Bolognese, which she really liked. It might be better if I spent one month with Dad and the next with Mum. Then there would be time to be normal without all this pressure for 'Deep and Meaningfuls'. The problem with that is Mum lets me do more or less what I like on Friday and Saturday nights and I don't think Dad would, he's so fussy. That's another thing they yell at one another over – when I get back late to Dad's on Saturday nights even though Mum's said it's okay for me to be late. Dad hardly ever goes to bed before one anyway.

Guess what!! When Dad took Matt and me to the Billy Joel concert two weeks ago he brought a friend with him. A woman!!! I was quite surprised. I hope he's not going to get into anything mushy, I don't think I could stand it. He's not the type.

When are you going to write to me?? I know you have written to David, but he won't show me the letter.

Your friend, Brook

Dear Donna

Your letter came last week and I've already read it a million times. The photos of the boat and your flat are great. And Heikko, what a gorgeous looking guy. If there are any more like that I'll be on the next plane!!! I think he sounds almost as nice as Matthew. I'm not surprised your Mum won't let him go with you when you are baby-sitting, especially when she caught you kissing in the lift. My Mum would have freaked and probably Dad would have grounded me. What sort of kisses does he do? You are lucky to be in the fourth form. It would have been slack being in with all the thirteen year old babies when you are nearly fifteen. It sounds like hard work though getting used to a different system. Your biology teacher sounds dreamy. You'll be able to listen to all his old Bob Dylan records when you baby-sit. Has he got any Dire Straits ones?

I'm going to spend the Easter break with Mum. And why??? Just listen to this. Dad is going on holiday with Judy, the woman who came to Billy Joel with us! It's getting serious. He'll be bringing her round here for the night next. And what's worse is that she has two sons. I hope they realize that there isn't enough room here for all of us. Just think of having to share with two boys. Groan!! Mum says I'm imagining things, but I'm not. I've got to do something. If she comes for the night I'll spew and if she comes for dinner I'll give her something horrible.

Matthew and I have talked for hours about it, he thinks it might be serious too and that there would be room at his house if I wanted to go there. I feel a bit mixed up at the moment. Dad seems so busy and is out a lot so I don't have time to talk to him much. I wish people would tell me what's going on. I'm not a baby. I'm very mature for my age if I'm given a chance. I don't feel like writing letters so that's it for this time.

Lots of love, Brook

Dear Donna

What a misery I was in my last letter. Your postcard cheered me up just when I needed it. Last week of term. Hurrah!

Emma, Rachel and I played a really good trick on Flit. I went up to her just before lunch break and asked her if she would give me back my watch. She had been looking after it for me during P.E. She said she didn't have it and she must have put it in the staff-room cupboard for safe-keeping. In the first period after lunch I went to Emma and Rachel's class because Flit was taking them for maths. I asked her if she'd found my watch and she said, No, was I sure I'd given it to her as she couldn't remember anything about it? Rachel and Emma came up to the front and backed me up. Emma reminded her that she'd put it on her wrist instead of in her pocket because it was so valuable. And then Rachel told her how it had been the last thing my Grandad had given me before he died and I began to sniff a bit. Flit looked really worried and upset and the other two took me to the door because I was crying by now and the whole class was looking uncomfortable. When we got outside the door Rachel put her head back in and said, 'April Fool, Miss Fletcher.' And we ran. You should have heard them laugh. Flit put her head on her arms and laughed so much they didn't do any more maths. When she saw me in the corridor later she said, 'You little monsters, just you wait!' but she was grinning. Matthew had already heard about it by the time school finished, he said it was all round the school.

I was right about Dad. He told me that he wants to marry Judy. He says that I'm growing up and that one day he'll be on his own. He really likes Judy and says that good women don't grow on trees. He didn't tell me before because he wanted to be sure first. So we have been out together a few times and Judy has been round to our place. She's quite nice, she listens a lot but doesn't say much to me. She brought me a book last time she came. I've also met her two sons. Gary is sixteen and quite good looking. Glen is twelve and a pain. Gary lives with his Dad, I'm not sure why. Glen lives with Judy and will be living with us. Just my luck. Why couldn't it have been the other way round. I've always wanted an older brother. They are planning to get married in May sometime because they can both take holidays then. As long as I don't have to share a room with Glen I don't mind. I couldn't bear to have some untidy kid messing up my room. I need somewhere of my own. He'll have to sleep in the sunroom.

Dad says we can all plan the wedding together. He wants us to be part of it, me and Glen that is. I just hope I'm not around when he tells Mum. Somehow I don't think she's going to be thrilled. It's funny, I hated the way they were always arguing and doing gross things to each other, but I still sometimes wish they would get back together. I think Mum is a good woman anyway.

Mum says Matthew can come over and stay with us over Easter. He likes Mum. I think it's because she goes to bed about 9 o'clock each night and then we can lie on the sofa together and watch TV. She gets annoyed with us if we giggle and laugh too much because it disturbs her. You'd think she'd be pleased to think that we weren't doing anything we shouldn't! Parents are odd. I'm going to be quite different when I'm a mother, that's for sure. Matt and I are going to have a party at Mum's too. Lots of videos, music and some decent drink. The guys are going to camp on the grass in the back garden and the girls will be inside. At least that's the idea!! David and Rachel are really going strong. Yours must have been the sort of young love that doesn't last. Matt is going to give me a gold ring when Dad gets married.

Got to go. Dad's yelling for me to hurry up. How's the handsome Heikko???

Dear Donna

Things certainly happen fast around here. Dad and Judy got married the first Saturday in May. It was in the morning at home, and afterwards we had this big buffet lunch. It was really quick. They just said that they promised to love and cherish each other, gave each other rings, then signed a piece of paper and they were married. I handed Dad the ring for Judy, and Glen did the same for his Mum. One of Judy's friends got so drunk he couldn't get up off the chair. He just sat and sat after everyone else had gone until his friend took him home. It was embarrassing. One of the little kids let the back door slam in the wind and there was glass everywhere and Judy tried to clean it up but didn't know where the broom was. Now Judy and Glen are living with us. Glen is sleeping in the sunroom.

I'm not sure I'm going to like this new life. Judy is dead keen that we should all be one big happy family. The other weekend we all had to go to Kuring-ai Park for the most excruciating picnic. Dad wouldn't let me ask Matthew because he said I needed to get to know Glen. (I know Glen all right. He's the nuthead who borrows my toothbrush when he can't find his and takes my hi-lighter and says he hasn't. He's so disorganized.) So we sat in the sun and ate greasy chicken. There was nothing else to do, so I just sat on the rug and picked the bits off it. Then Dad started to rouse on me and said don't just sit there, go and play with Glen. For heaven's sake, I'm not a little girl! And all this time Dad and Judy are gazing at one another and giggling at nothing at all, just as if I wasn't there. It's hideous at their age. And next weekend they want to take us to Wonderland. Honestly, I feel like a kid again. I don't think even Glen wants to go.

Right now I'm baby-sitting Glen instead of ice-skating with the others because it's Dad's birthday and he's gone out to dinner. It's not fair on a Saturday night. Last year I made chilli con carne and put flowers and candles on the table. It looked really good. This year it's Judy Judy Judy and I get landed with Glen. He's watching Rambo for about the hundredth time, what a creephead. Matthew is coming round in a few minutes, I hope. He's being doing great at basketball. He thinks he may get chosen for the state team if he practises a bit more. The netball team is doing well too. Rachel is in it, but she's not as good as you at shooting. We haven't lost a single match so far.

Dad says I might be able to go to Hong Kong next year in the July holidays. Isn't that great????? We could go on that ferry you were telling me about and maybe camp at Ham Tin. I'd like to see that rock you've all been jumping off. Did you win the butterfly and the freestyle in the Age Groups? It's getting too cold to swim here. Here's Matt. He says hello.

Brook

Dear Don-the-Dan-eater

Hey, great to get your letter and to hear all about Dan.
Sorry to hear Heikko turned out to be such a jerk. I'm
glad his boat sank in his first race, it must have looked
really funny. Dan sounds like a bit of a nutcase, lots of
fun. He looks quite serious in the photo. I like his eyes. I
thought they'd be slanty, but they are really big. Tell me
how he's different from Australian guys, you know what
I mean!!!!! Matt and I are still going strong, but
sometimes I have this funny feeling that it can't last.
We've had a few arguments lately and he gets all quiet.
But then it's okay again. Term finishes at the end of next
week. I can't wait.

Melissa has been suspended. You know Michael has
been really hot for her for ages. He gave her this great
watch and told her that he'd bought it with the money
he earned working at Coles on Saturdays. Any idiot
could have told that it was more expensive than that and
I know he's been hanging around with George, and he's
on probation. Melissa's mother came and talked to old
Fruit-face and when he asked Melissa about it, you
should have heard her. She went mad. She was
screaming and yelling at Fruit-face and her Mum and
then she told Fruit-face it was none of his bloody
business what she did outside school and he could bog
off and leave her alone. Fruit-face nearly bust a gut, he
went red all the way up to his ears. Melissa's Mum didn't

know what to do, I felt sorry for her. I don't know whether Melissa will be back next term or not. She may go to live with her father in Queensland. Michael is in deep strife with the police but they'll be easy on him because he's never been in trouble before. His Dad's furious and has grounded him for a month. Matthew thinks Michael's father lets him do what he likes too much of the time and should do more things with him. It's a bit late for that at his age!

Matt got into the basketball team. He's going off for a week's basketball clinic, so I won't see much of him. He spends most of Saturday practising and on Sundays he often helps his Dad. They are building a new house and he gets $50 for a day's work. He's saving up for a car. He wants a Torana because they have power and beauty he says. The engine that is! They look boring I think.

We are moving house on the eighteenth of July. We are going to a place called Gymea in the south. Judy works in Wollongong and they have decided that it would be best if they lived halfway. There are times when I hate that woman and her lousy son. They pretend that they are consulting us, but really they aren't. You know they are just trying to be nice, and that we will move anyway. What about Matthew? What about my schooling? Don't they know it's bad to shift in the middle of year nine? I said I'd stay with Mum, then I wouldn't need to change schools, but I heard Judy saying that Mum drinks too much and Dad should keep an eye on me as I was going through a period of adjustment. What does she know about it, she's only known me for three

16

months. Dad just does whatever she says. Gymea is full of nerds anyway. If I have to spend weekends with Mum I'll never make friends in Gymea. At least I'd be with Matthew.

I know Judy tries but why did Dad have to marry her? Couldn't they have just been friends? We were doing fine without her. She wants me to be a child again she says. It's not right for me to be looking after Dad, doing the washing and cooking. I should be playing!!!! Little does she realize how grown-up I am, and how impossible it is to turn the clock back. She hates the way the kitchen is organized but I took her round it when she first moved in and told her that this was how Mum had always had things, that we put the biscuits for Dad in a special place and that no one else was allowed to touch them. She looked everywhere for the garlic squeezer last night and never thought of looking in with the tools. She had to use a knife instead, serve her right. She thinks I don't know how to make spaghetti. I'm just a baby. I'm not even allowed to use the phone in Dad's bedroom any more, I have to use the one in the kitchen when I talk to Matthew. They are impossible sometimes. And when I do go into their room it has a different smell. Mum always used to smell of flowers mixed with a sort of fruity smell from the grog, but Judy smells all sort of peppery, it makes you want to sneeze.

Next time you write you'd better use our new address. The house isn't bad. It looks over the water and Dad says we'll maybe have a sailboard. It's quite near the National Park – no more picnics, I hope – and only ten minutes away from the beach. Cronulla is a dump compared with Palm Beach though. Dad says life's a challenge, it sure is, especially with Judy and Glen around. Write again soon. I need your letters. Love and all that,

Brook

Dear Donna

Here we are in Gorgeous Gymea right down in the south of Sydney and it's freezing. The house is high up, a bit like a tree-house, and the wind whips round it. It's what Dad calls cladding, which means that all the heat zaps through the walls. No longer is there a bubble of warm air surrounding us when we get up in the morning. Looking out over the water is quite good though, and I've taken some good photos of sunsets. The cats love the garden and have discovered how to get up on the roof. Dill climbs over the roof, shins down onto the balcony and then yowls to be let in because he can see us. Glen and I have bedrooms opposite each other, both quite small. Dad's is next to mine and then there is a big living room with a sunroom sort of off it but still part of it. There's an excellent room under the house, but Dad says they want it for a study and maybe Glen will have it when he's older. Just because he's a boy. I suppose they can't trust me. I might get pregnant!!! I'm going to paint my room gold and I'm getting new doona covers and everything. Dad's going to put up bookshelves and a row of cupboards for me to put my stereo on. I might even persuade him to let me have his TV now we've got Judy's as well.

There's some shops at the top of the road and a shopping centre called Westwall not far away. It's got a bowling alley where everyone meets after school and at weekends. There are pin-ball machines and all the latest video games. The woman who runs it kicks people out if they don't do as she says, but a lot of the kids are on drugs there, so she has to be pretty rough with them. There's also a roller-skating rink at Cronulla. It's new and they have a good club there, no ice-skating though. Aren't you impressed at what I've found out in two short weeks? Matthew came over last weekend and Dad gave me some money to go out to dinner. We went to a Chinese restaurant, it was unreal. It was covered with mirrors, dragons and lanterns and things like that and the food was great. Matt looked great too in his black and grey striped shirt. I felt proud of him, especially when we passed some of the kids from school on our way there. When Dad gave me the money Judy gave him that look which means she doesn't approve. I bet she thinks I'm not old enough to have dinner with a boy. Safety in numbers she says. Lucky for me Dad thinks different.

You wouldn't believe how Judy has changed now we are in this house. She's so tidy for one thing, and wants us all to be too. The bathroom towels live on the bottom shelf in the hall cupboard, who has put them on the top shelf?? As if it matters. And if I take a clean one without asking, you should hear the fuss. It's okay if darling Glen takes one, of course. Today Glen asked her if he could borrow her comb and she said yes, when only yesterday she said no when I asked her. We've got lots of her furniture from her old house and she's always running round wiping off marks or cracking up if we put our feet on the table. I don't know if I can stand it. And we have to sit up at table, no TV, and no rude comments when we eat. How will she ever know what I like if I can't say? I don't think Dad likes it much either, especially having to wash-up straight after dinner instead of later on. The worst thing is that I think she wants to be my Mum. She's started to tell me what to do, what clothes I should wear for school, when I should do my homework, what TV I can watch, and even what sort of sandwiches I should eat!! As if I can't run my own life. Perhaps it's escaped her notice that I have always been in the top groups at school and don't need help with deciding when to do my homework. Maybe I'll leave one of my school reports lying around where she can see it. And after all this she wants to give me a hug and expects me to hug her back. When I don't she goes all quiet and then later on I can hear her and Dad talking in their bedroom and I bet it's about me. But I've got my own Mum, I don't want another one. Maybe some kids do, but I don't.

I miss going to Mum's. I hope she's okay. She phones nearly everyday but it's not the same. Dad says they think it's better for me to spend the first month here without going back to North Sydney, that way I'll consolidate my life here, whatever he thinks that means! I know I was moaning about living in two places, but it's pretty hideous having all these decisions made for me. I can just hear Judy saying that Dad has got better things to do than driving me back to Mum's each night and that means living here and going to school here. Sometimes I feel so helpless being only fourteen. I'm not a parcel that can be sent any old place.

School's not bad. There are some quite good-looking boys in year ten and eleven. The girls are real tarts. They've got too much make-up and their skirts are so short you can see their undies. You wouldn't be allowed to look like that at Kuring-ai. They all hang around at recess and smoke behind the boys' toilets. There are two in my maths class who seem okay. It will be better when we start netball and gym again. There's a great drama club here and I've joined that. Wait for the next instalment of this gripping drama, what new events will befall the intrepid heroine as she battles this crazy shifting world created by even crazier adults.

Write soon, love,
     Brook

Dear Donna

Thanks for your letter. I miss you even more now I'm down in this dead-end place. Dad says to give it time, but there's no one I can really talk to here. For a bit I rang Emma or Rachel each night and that helped, but then Judy started moaning about the phone bill and how no one else could use the phone. Not that I've noticed her having all that many calls. You know how Mum always calls each evening even if it's only for a minute or two? Well, she's not allowed to do that any more. Dad thinks it upsets Judy and calls it an intrusion. Sometimes I get mad at him when he does things like that. If they mind so much why not have a second phone down in the study, that would be ace, but it's too much money! Everything is. So now I can't use the phone after nine o'clock and not more than fifteen minutes at a time and I'm allowed to phone Mum once a week. Hey, it would be good to ring you, put your number in your next letter. I liked the photos of Sunset Peak with the little cabins and all that mist. That's the sort of holiday I'd like, playing wild games all over the peak in the mist. Sort of spooky but exciting, especially with Dan there as well.

I've only seen Matthew once since I last wrote, and that was last weekend. It's difficult getting together because he has the basketball most Saturdays and Sundays and I'm not allowed to leave here because of us being one big happy family! We went roller-skating. Being able to ice-skate helped quite a bit, but you should see my bruises. I've got a huge one on my hip, all purple, yellow and blue. Matthew wasn't any better than me so we didn't stay long. Matt spent the night, he shared Glen's room, not mine unfortunately! The next day we took our bikes down to the National Park. It's really steep there, we were going faster than the cars in some places. I love the feeling of freedom and speed · and the wind through my hair. I wished it would go on for ever. We ended up at some beach where we lay in the sun for ages. I told Matt how miserable I was and even cried it was so bad. He held me for ages and said all the right things, he knows just what I need. Then a whole lot of other people arrived so we started for home.

Judy had made this huge dinner with chops and lots of other disgustingly fatty stuff. It was just swimming in grease and I could hardly eat any of it. Judy began to look as though she'd swallowed a prune stone and Dad told me to stop making a fuss or leave the table. In front of Matthew! He knows I can't eat that stuff, he could have backed me up instead of making things worse. So everything fell apart and then it was time for Matt to go home and I felt like crying again. I think Judy did too, I don't know why. Why does she always want me to be grateful for everything? She's always wanting us to thank her. Dad's getting good at it but it just sticks in my throat like a lump and I can't get the words out even when I sometimes want to.

Next weekend I'm going to Mum's and Matt will be there. It will be so excellent, I can't wait.

Love, Brook

Dear Donna

Here I am at Gran's for two weeks. It's just so great to be away from school and I can forget all about Glen and Judy. I love the mountains at this time of year and I adore staying with Gran. On Sunday we got up early and walked up to the German cake shop. It was freezing, we could see our breath in the air ahead of us. Then inside the shop it was warm and smelled delicious. We sat and had croissants and coffee and lots of people came and talked to us. Some of them I remembered from last time. We took bread and a nutty cake home with us. I picked bits off the bread all the way home. Yum! Next day Gran showed me how to make scones and we started on our Christmas cake. She told me that when she was young and making her first Christmas cake she put in two pounds of carrots instead of two ounces and then, because they were poor and she didn't want to waste anything, she decided to put ten times all the other ingredients in as well. She said it just got bigger and bigger until she ended up having enough mixture to fill a huge washing-up bowl and Granpa wasn't a bit pleased. And then he had to eat it all himself because she was pregnant with Dad and didn't feel like cake. They made puddings too and kept some in metal tins for the next year, but when they went to get it the tins were all lacy where the pudding had eaten its way through. She's a great cook now though.

We have been gardening in the mornings and then

going for bush walks in the afternoon. Because it's spring everything is beginning to grow so we are putting manure all over the garden. I'm very useful because Gran has a bad back. There are flowers everywhere, it has been a warm winter Gran says. Feels cold to me. Gran put some daffodils in my room to greet me and we have hyacinths and jonquils in pots in the sitting room. They smell so good. I can see the sun shining on the cherry blossom when I lie in bed in the morning and the king parrots swooping through the trees. If you feed them sweet stuff it is like giving kids junk food. They love it but it does something to stop their feathers growing strong. We give them seeds mostly. We are going to see the camellia gardens at the weekend. I can't decide which I like best, camellias or roses. Yesterday we went to Lyrebird's Dell and then down to the Pool of Siloam, do you remember that from last summer when you stayed with us? We took a picnic lunch and then found a place in the sun and read for a bit. I'm going to do the Govett's leap and Bridal Veil Falls walk with some friends of Gran's next week. She wants to burn off some of my energy!!!!

I even love it when the weather is bad up here. I love lighting the fire and curling up with a book on the sofa or just looking at the flames. Gran thinks I must have been a cat in my last life. Cinnamon remembered me and follows me round the garden just like a dog but she likes it best when I'm reading. I haven't written any other letters. I don't even feel like phoning Matthew. Gran thinks I need some space. I've talked to her quite a lot. Judy is like a black whirlwind changing everything in its path. Dad's like a storm cloud but Gran's like cool rain on a summer's day.

It's much easier to think about things at a distance. Gran says stepfamilies are hard work for everyone. Each person has a bag of ideas as to how things should be done, and inside each bag is different. It's like throwing the contents all in a heap in the middle and then choosing what's best for this family, a bit from here and a bit from there. The trouble is that Judy wants us to choose all the things in her bag. Gran and I think taking one idea at a time and trying it out would be good. And maybe Judy, Dad, Glen and me each having a turn at choosing.

We are now going out to a craft place at Katoomba where I'm going to buy some presents for Matthew, Emma and Rachel. I'll write again soon.

Lots of love,
Brook

Dear Donna

Another letter from you just when I need it. Your timing
is excellent. I wouldn't have guessed that Hong Kong
had pubs like that. They sound better than here. I liked
the bit about the sailor saying you'd made his evening
by just being there. Did you give him one of your looks
or did Dan whip you away before you had the chance?
I can't wait until next year. It will be so great.

It's been really warm since I got back from Gran's.
I've been doing up my surf board with Barb from my
Geography group. It's great. We went down to one of
the surf board shops in Cronulla and asked them how to
do it and what to use. You should have seen us. We went
on our bikes, taking it in turns to hold the board. The
wind almost blew us over in some places. I thought Barb
was going to get smashed by a car. We've turned the
garage into a workshop and I'm halfway through
patching the holes with fibre glass. Dad and Judy don't
bother us, they think it is keeping us occupied. We've
fixed up a light and a radio by running a lead from the
house. Hope it doesn't rain.

I'm at Mum's for the weekend. We've got a new
system. I told you they were planning something! I
spend three out of four weekends here and the weeks
with Dad. It's a drag in some ways because of missing
netball but it means I can see Matthew. He had his
seventeenth birthday just before I went to Gran's. I
gave him a U2 album. He really liked it. We had a

birthday dinner at his place with his Mum, Dad and Jenny. It was fun, we even had sparklers for Jenny, and some wine in tall glasses. Then Matt and I went out to a movie. We saw *Beverley Hills Cop*. It was ace. Eddie Murphy is really cool. The car chase was unreal. Afterwards we hung around for a bit and then, wait for it, Matt drove me back to Mum's!!!!!!! He passed his test first go and is allowed to use his Mum's car. We sat in it for ages saying goodnight. I had to tear myself away in the end when I saw Mum's light go on. What an evening! It was past one o'clock when I got to bed.

I got back from Gran's feeling great and ready to try to make things work at home. I walked in and started to tell Dad about the last two weeks and then I noticed this list on the fridge. You should see it. It says when I have to do things like clean up my room and wash-up. I hate it, it makes me feel so stupid. What bugs me is that they don't discuss things with me, they decide and then tell me. Grrr!!!! Obviously Judy has been getting at Dad and they gave me this long lecture about chores and house rules. It was okay the way it was before, in my opinion. Then we did the things that needed doing, when they needed doing. None of this garbage about rules. I hate it when Judy tells me what to do. She has this special high little voice when she talks to me. She thinks she's being friendly, but it's sickly sweet. Yuk! Yuk! Yuk! The other day I went into their bedroom to ask Dad for my pocket money and the fuss! Now I'm shut out of their bedroom. I can't use the long mirror in there unless I ask first. I know just why she likes me going to Mum's for the weekend, specially when Glen goes to his Dad's. You should hear them sometimes, it's pretty hard to take and it's disgusting at their age anyway. They think I don't know what they are up to, they're so naive it's pathetic.

Last weekend was a rage. Emma, Rachel and I went to Palm Beach in the morning. We walked across to Pittwater and mucked around there for a bit then went back to the shops to meet Matt and the others. When we got there Rachel had left her new shorts and towel at the other beach. We all ran back as fast as we could, scrambling over the rocks because the tide was coming up. It took for ever and we got mega wet on the way back because the waves were crashing on the rocks. Result was that we missed the five o'clock movie, so we decided to go and have something to eat at the place where the ferries come in. It's a great place. People playing guitars and trombones, trick cyclists and a man who was pretending to be a black Sambo doll with jerky movements. You could hardly tell he was a real man. Then we went to Darling Harbour. The shops there are like Aladdin's cave. We were having such a good time that we missed the seven o'clock showing of our film. We raced up the road to the cinema and ran till our legs gave out, but we couldn't make it. I tried to ring Dad to tell him I wouldn't be in at seven, but he wasn't there. We went down to the video games place in George Street and had an excellent time. You have to watch out for thieves though, they can pick your pocket without you feeling a thing. In the end we went to the nine-thirty show and saw *Top Gun*. I got a great Tom Cruise poster. He's such an ace guy. Matt drove me back but we didn't get home until after midnight. I don't think I've ever seen Dad so mad. He shouted at Matthew and told him to take himself off and he grounded me for two weeks. Groan. After all, I did try to ring him. It wasn't my fault that he was out. Just as well Judy didn't poke her nose into it or I think I would have exploded. I was so tired all I wanted to do was get into bed. So I've got to put up with lame-brain Glen for another whole weekend. Pity me.

Love, Brook

Dear Donna

Surprise! Surprise! Bet you never expected to hear from me again so soon. Thanks for the card, but most of all for the black silk pants. I just love them. I look mega sexy in them and they feel all soft and clinging. Judy gave me a red shirt that goes really well with the pants, although it hasn't got quite the same class. Dad gave me a watch with a gold band to replace the one that was stolen from my bag at school. It's great. It has a little gold chain on it in case it comes undone. That idiot Glen gave me a box of three toothbrushes because he says I'm so fussy about him using mine. He's the one who needs them, not me!! Matt came over on my birthday and gave me a little silver locket with his picture in it. It's real cute. Some of the girls from school came over and we mostly ate and watched videos all evening. It was good fun, and the others like Matt. He's getting to know some of them quite well now. Mum was upset because she wasn't there. Usually she makes the cake and Dad does the rest and we all get together at her place or Dad's. They say they can suspend their differences for one day a year. But now Judy's around Dad gets all protective of her and then Mum either goes mad or cries. I really hate it when she calls Dad names. I read somewhere that every arrow a parent fires at the other parent goes straight through the heart of a child, and I know just what that means. Almost forgot to say that Mum gave me a great book called Space Demons and a U2 record and we watched *The Pink Panther* on Mum's VCR. I wish Dad would get one instead of just borrowing the one from work, but Judy says she doesn't want Glen spending all his time watching horror movies.

We've had great dramas here. Yesterday the garage burned down! Judy had been walking round all morning with her nose twitching saying she could smell smoke from bush fires. Glen's cigs more likely! Anyway, she was hanging out the washing when she gave this great yell and we rushed out to see black smoke pouring from the garage. Judy grabbed her car keys and moved her car from the car port. It's a Mazda RXL and she loves it. I thought it would be a good idea if Dad left his old wreck there and then he could get a new one, but he moved his too. Glen and I fixed up the hose but by the time we got it there the flames were huge and were spurting through the roof, and the lousy trickle of water was hopeless. All the neighbours came out in a panic with their hoses. They were scared the bush would catch fire and all their houses would go up in flames. So we all tried to keep the garage roof cool and the bush wet with everyone shouting and telling each other what to do. The fire engine took ages to come, but they said it was only 12 minutes. It took no time to put it out. Lots of things hadn't actually burned but were all black or soggy from the water. Dad had a canoe from the Solomons in the garage so he was pretty upset about that. The first thing I saw when I went in was the hind legs and bum of the old rocking horse. It's funny, but I minded much more about that than about my wet suit and my surf board. It was part of my past I guess. Dad says we are insured so we will get a new garage, but nothing can bring back my old rocking horse.

Judy asked the firemen how they thought it started and told them that I'd been resurfacing my surfboard and that I'd been using acetone and resin. She didn't actually say it was my fault but somehow she made me feel awful. She always blames me for everything that goes wrong and thinks Glen is so perfect. And she's always right whatever happens. Sometimes it would be great to have Dad back me up, but he thinks taking sides is wrong and we should sort it out ourselves. It's so different from before, when we could talk about everything. I'm sure it wasn't anything to do with the surfboard. Barb and I were really careful with the tins of stuff because we knew they were highly flammable. We always put the tops on and didn't leave the rags around either. There was a lot of junk on the garage floor though and all Dad's old newspapers and books and our firewood and brickettes. The other thing is that I know Glen goes up there to smoke and I'm always telling him to stub out his butts and not to just throw them down to burn out. I didn't know whether to say anything as Judy doesn't know her darling boy smokes and Dad gets cranky if I say anything nasty about Glen. He really likes Glen. He says he always wanted a son and a daughter, so Glen can do no wrong. Glen's lucky because Dad's much easier to get along with than Judy is. He isn't so particular about trivial details. Glen's just had braces on his teeth and he looks hideous. It's made his words sound all fluffy too. Dad says he'll get used to them in no time. Huh! I hope he doesn't.

That's all the news for now. Will write again soon. Love and all that.

Brook

Dear Donna

Something really awful has happened. I can hardly bear it. Matthew has been seen out with another girl. I've asked Emma and Rachel about it and they said that they've had their suspicions for quite a while. I haven't seen much of him lately because of the basketball and his work on his Dad's house. So I thought!!! What am I going to do? I feel as if my heart is broken and I have a whole lot of sharp pieces inside me. It hurts so much. Why didn't he tell me? We could have talked about it. I don't know whether to ring him up or what. Dad and Judy keep on at me to tell them what's wrong, but I don't know how to. Last month I wrote Matt a letter and told him I couldn't go all the way with him. I don't know why, but I just couldn't. I don't think I'm ready, it's too scary, even with Matthew. He said that he loved me for myself, not just my body and that it was okay. It wouldn't make any difference to us, he could wait. And now he's going out with someone else. Guys are all the same it seems to me.

To make matters worse, Mum has got a boyfriend. When I arrived yesterday he was here. I went to bed really early because I was so miserable, and when I went to say goodnight to Mum she said not to come into her room in the morning. I said why not, and she said she'd be with John. Honestly, I felt sick. So I went off to bed without saying anything and then a few minutes later she came in and asked if I was upset. Well, what do you think? So then she gave me this long lecture on how she deserved some fun in life and she couldn't go on putting me first for ever (as if she ever did) and ended up by saying it was the same as what Matthew and I were doing. So I just said it was quite different and if she couldn't see that, I didn't want to talk about it. This is the worst weekend of my life. Honestly, I don't think anyone cares about me at all, they're all too busy with their own problems, or each other, to even notice me. Mum didn't even think to ask why I was going to bed so early or if I was okay, all she wanted to talk about was John.

Please write soon. I'm desperate.
Brook

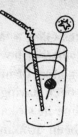

Dear Donna

Your letter really helped and talking to you on the phone
was so great. It saved my life. Tell Dan that I appreciated
having his point of view too. Last week I threw the
locket Matthew gave me off the balcony into the bushes.
That's called a symbolic gesture!! But it's hard when
everyone around me has someone special. Mum's acting
all mushy with John, Dad's got Judy, and everyone at
school is going with someone. Deborah told me that the
others think I'm a snob because I come from the North
Shore and that's why the boys won't go out with me.
Who'd want to go out with that bunch of jerks anyway.

Things have been mega bad here recently. Dad and
Judy have been lecturing me or having these great D
and Ms which end up with them doing the talking and
me staring at the carpet wishing I could disappear. They
always have an answer for everything, and they are so
dumb that they haven't realized Matt and I have broken
up. Actually, I think Judy has guessed, but I wouldn't
tell her in a million years. It's none of her business.
Why does she always have to appear on the scene just
when I've got Dad to myself? She's got no tact. And
then the phone bill arrived! Our call cost $90, but to
hear them go on about it you'd think it was $900 at
least. I've got to pay it back out of my allowance and if
I ring you again I won't be allowed to visit you in July.
Glen rings his friends all the time and he doesn't have
to pay anything. This is my weekend at home, and what

does Dad do? He takes Glen to a cricket match. I'm beginning to wonder whether he still loves me at all.

I've been spending most of my time around at Debbie's place. She's been having an awful time with her father. Some of the time he's okay, in fact he tells great jokes, but when he's been drinking he freaks out really easily and then he bashes her up. He's out most of the time though. Her mum is great. She's good to talk to and understands what you are on about. She really likes me and says I can stay any time. Sometimes when Deb's mum is out and her dad is working, one of the boys gets a few videos and we all sit around and share a bong. Have you tried them? They're great. It makes you feel as if you are floating in space and you say really clever things and everything seems so funny. (Actually, I've only tried it once and I felt gross later on. Maybe that's what Mum feels like when she says she is hung-over. No wonder she gets so cranky.) The other thing some of them do is to grind some stuff into a powder and then mix it with sleeping pills and uppers. You need a scrip for most of those things, so they aren't easy to get. They mix that up with lemonade and drink it with beer and then they go off the air waves. It's no fun being with them then. I think they are nutcases. Most of Deb's friends have really mega problems at school or at home, that's why they do it. But they don't realize how dangerous it is, it could kill you. And it doesn't solve their problems either, it just makes them forget for a bit so that they don't need to try and sort things out. Dad would go off his head if he knew. Specially as he's always going on about communicating.

I think even breathing in that white stuff is affecting me. I can't seem to remember things very well, they slide around in my head and then they're gone. I sit there looking out of the window thinking about living on the North Shore and Matthew and I don't care whether I get good marks or not. The teachers are all on my back and Dad is cracking up about it. He's started nagging me about my homework and keeps asking me do I have any assignments to do. Next thing he'll be telling me I haven't got time to write to you! At least Judy is more sensible, she told him my school work is my responsibility. He didn't like that and they started to argue. But it *is* my life and I'm going to live it how I want to, not how everyone else thinks I should. Judy is right. All I want is freedom to do things my way.

Please write soon,
Brook

Dear Donna

I don't know what I'd do if I couldn't write all my
thoughts and feelings to you. Life hasn't looked up much
since I last wrote. I couldn't wait to get away to Mum's
place this weekend. At least it's peaceful. Mum's been
so busy, I've hardly seen her recently. Rachel, Emma
and I went into Chatswood today and bought our
Christmas presents. The shops are crowded but it was
fun. Mum gave me some extra money and has organized
for me to help a friend of hers in her shop up till
Christmas Eve. I'm going to spend Christmas here with
Mum and John. It's so much better than at home.

The second last week of term was the pits. I lost my
house key and when I came home after school Glen
had taken off with the spare one we keep in the laundry.
I looked everywhere for him, but the little creep had
gone off to a friend's house. I tried all the windows, they
usually leave one unlocked somewhere and I can climb
in. If I remember to put the ladder away they never
know. I was desperate because I'd promised Debbie I'd
meet her down at the bowling alley and then we were
going to hang around and play the videos. Her
boyfriend was bringing his friend. In the end I climbed
up onto the roof and took three of the tiles off and
squeezed in that way. I was filthy by the time I'd crawled
to the trap door leading into the corridor. Then I had
to put the ladder away and have a shower. I got there
just as they were leaving. Craig's friend is called Scott.

He seemed quite okay. He's a roller-skating nut. We went to Maccers, then to a movie and on to Debbie's place. By this time it was about midnight and I was getting worried about what Dad would say. It was also pouring with rain and I didn't feel like walking home and I didn't think Dad would come and get me. About half-past twelve Dad arrived. I got the shock of my life. He was mega, mega furious. I'd forgotten all about those bloody tiles. They were sitting watching TV when the ceiling started to drip, and then trickle and then pour. It sounded so funny I started to laugh and Dad slapped me, just once. It was hideous. He told Debbie she was a bad influence on me and that she wasn't welcome at our house any more. We just sat in the car without saying anything on the way home. He said he'd talk to me in the morning.

Next day I got up really early and left for school before breakfast! I didn't see Judy or Dad. Glen was there with a smirk on his face of course. When I got to school there was Debbie with a black eye and great big bruises on her arm. You could actually see the finger marks where her dad had grabbed her. He's an animal. She had a whole lot of money and said she was going to run away. I said I'd go with her so we went back to Dad's place and I got some clothes and took $50 and my bankbook out of Dad's desk. Then we caught the train up to Taree, where Debbie's uncle has a cabin. It took a long time to get there and there was a gross man sitting near us. He had a bottle of booze and kept giving out these enormous belches. I was beginning to wish I hadn't come but Debbie thought we'd feel better when we got to the cabin. We planned to eat, spend the night and then hitch up to Surfers Paradise and find somewhere to stay. There are lots of cheap places there. When we got out at Taree there were two policemen standing on the platform. Debbie tried to duck out under the fence but they saw her and asked her what her name was. They had been looking for us because Debbie's mother had told them about her brother's cabin.

It was so embarrassing at first. I felt like a criminal. But it was exciting driving back to Sydney in the police car. The driver put his siren on a couple of times and you should have seen people get out of the way. I was hoping he'd have to chase someone but he said his job was to get us back to Sydney. They were great. We even stopped for something to eat on the way. When we got back to the police station we had to go and see the sergeant and he showed us a gross book full of photographs of girls who had gone missing and had not been seen for months or years. By the time Dad came to get me I was so relieved to see him that I didn't care how angry he was.

When we got home Judy was there and she burst into tears when she saw me. It was even more embarrassing than the police. She gave me a big hug and brought me a milkshake when I was in bed. She told me not to worry, just to have a good sleep and we'd work things out in the morning, and that Dad was more upset than angry. Sometimes that woman surprises me. You wouldn't believe how long I slept. I was totally wrecked. All I did all weekend was sleep and eat. In the end Judy and Dad went up to the school to see the counsellor and I talked to her too. She was okay and told me that I was responsible for my own life. Not news to me!!! Anyway, I told Dad and Judy about Matthew and we talked for ages and agreed that I would spend Christmas with Mum, and then Judy and I would go up to Gran's for two weeks. Seems a funny idea but Gran says it's okay and that Dad will be spending the weekends and that we can all start afresh in the new year. Judy's other son will be spending Christmas with them, but they've promised not to let him have my room.

I hope you like your present. Your friend,
Brook

Dear Donna

Christmas is over and it wasn't anything like as bad as I
expected. I still miss Matthew, but now it's more like an
aching tooth. While I was at Mum's I went to a party
with Rachel and Emma. Half way through the evening
who should walk in but Matthew and this dark-haired
girl called Samantha. What a name. I nearly died, but I
wasn't going to let it get to me, so I acted real cool and
friendly. You would have been proud of me. Samantha
was mad at Matt and kept giving me these bitchy looks
and whispering behind her hand. What a cow. She hung
on to Matthew like a leech and wouldn't let him talk
to anyone for more than a minute or two. Matt couldn't
handle it and kept knocking back vodkas until he could
hardly stand. He was so loud it was slack. Then he
started chucking up and some friends took him home
I think. Samantha was fussing round him saying Oh
Matthew are you alright and silly things like that. Why
did I think he was so great? He's just the same as
everyone else, not special at all. Another illusion
shattered!!

Working in the shop was great. It was one of those
boutiques with sort of arty craft things as well. I was
supposed to be helping with the jewellery and dried
flowers but it was much more fun helping with the
clothes. The old bags would come out of the fitting rooms
and prance round looking at themselves in the

mirrors and saying Well, what do you think? You weren't
allowed to say that they looked gross. I got quite good
at saying things like I think the green suits you better.
Then they smiled at me and told Mum's friend what a
charming child I was. Enough to make you throw up.
Some of the customers weren't so old and knew exactly
what they wanted and were really rude. They used to
drop the clothes on the floor and leave them for us to pick
up. Sometimes there was lipstick on them too. I don't
know how Hannah stands it. She let me buy some of
the jewellery cheap, so I got some excellent earrings,
including the ones I sent you.

Christmas day was okay. Mum had a whole raft of
people round and was in one of her cooking moods so
there were about four great desserts. John was there
looking after the drinks. I quite like him, he doesn't
treat me like a child. When he poured the champagne
he gave me some without asking Mum. After lunch we
all slept for a bit and then, because it was so hot, we all
went off to Mona Vale. It was great getting into the
water. Didn't do much after that. Everyone went home
and then John and Mum began to get all moony and I
started to feel a bit sad. I don't know why, so I went off
to my room and played my new albums. I got a
Midnight Oil, a Billy Idol with Rebel Yell on it, and
a Eurythmics. I just love, 'Would I lie to you' and 'Here
comes the rain again'. I rang Dad before I went to bed
and he said they'd had a good day and that they'd
missed me.

I met a really spunky guy called Jason at the Boxing
Day party. He reminded me of Jason Donovan, but Emma
dragged me away. She's right. It's just too far, living in
Gymea. I don't want another Matthew. Why aren't

there any decent boys in Gymea? I went back to Dad's
for New Year. Gary was there. He's seventeen now and
is better looking than I remembered. He's in year eleven
and wants to go to Art School. Glen doesn't like him
at all because he can't get away with anything. Gary
even made Glen do the washing-up. Ha, Ha!! I wish I
knew how he does it. He's very quiet. The three of us
went to see *Crocodile Dundee*. It was really funny. You'd
love it. If it comes to Hong Kong you have to see it.
While I was home I tried to contact Debbie. I called
five times but nobody answered so I think they must be
away. I hope she's okay.

I talked a lot to Gary. I wondered why he doesn't
live with us. He said that Judy and his dad had hideous
fights and then wouldn't talk to each other for days.
Mostly about his dad being away so much. He's a musician
and has to travel or play late at night. Then no one
would do the shopping and there'd be nothing to eat
and no one would cook meals. Sounds gross. So then
Judy got a job and walked out on his dad. She took
Glen with her because he was only eight, but Gary said
he felt so sorry for his dad that he stayed with him.
There were fights over that too, Judy said he was too
young to be left on his own while his dad was away.
They even went to court about it and Gary was saved
by his Aunt who used to come in and look after him.
Now he's old enough to be left on his own and he says
his dad couldn't manage without him. He used to think
Judy was a bitch walking out like that. His dad was
shattered when it happened and used to cry every night
and Gary didn't understand or know what to do about
it. Now he's older he thinks he can see why Judy left
and how they weren't right for one another, but it still

makes him sad. He feels as though his childhood came to an end at thirteen. Judy used to put notes on the food in the fridge even then. 'Don't touch this trifle, it's for dinner tonight.'

Judy and I are up here with Gran. It's much cooler than Sydney. Gary and Glen are both spending two weeks with their father in Melbourne and Dad is finishing some writing he has to get done before term starts. I know it's their way of splitting me up from Debbie, but as I'm sure she's on holiday too I don't mind.

Write and tell me what you did in the hols and what you are doing with Dan. Happy New Year and love from

Brook

Dear Donna

It was great to get back here and find your letter waiting and also the photos. They're really excellent. It's not much fun only having two weeks' holiday at Christmas although you did a lot. You're so lucky learning to scuba dive. Isn't it cold in January? It's funny that you are doing a photography course because I'm going to do one next week. Judy suggested it while we were up in the Blue Mountains. Gary told her that I wished I could do some painting but I didn't think there'd be much point as I'm hopeless at drawing and he thought I might be good at photography. So I'm starting on Monday next week. It's black and white and we do our own developing and printing. I can't wait.

The Blue Mountains were great as usual. Gran and Judy got on like a house on fire, they never stopped talking and laughing. It turned out that they'd done lots of the same sort of things, like living in Singapore, Chinese painting, and sky diving!!! Honestly, can you imagine Gran jumping out of an aeroplane??? I didn't believe her, but she had some photos and dug them out to show us. I suppose she wasn't always old. They both like books and museums too. Different from Dad who likes all the outdoor things when he isn't writing. Judy said that when she was my age she did lots of sports and she'd forgotten how much fun it was. Maybe there's hope for her yet! We did some windsurfing on the lake. There wasn't much wind but it was fun anyway. Judy kept falling in. Naturally I was quite a bit better at it.

We went on the Scenic Railway, swimming in Springwood pool after walking for miles, and to this amazing old place that looks like a pink ice-cream and is so old-fashioned that it reminds you of *Gone with the Wind* somehow. All curtains and velvet. The view is fantastic. You look right over the bush and the mountains for miles and miles. It drops steeply just in front of the hotel. Gran doesn't like the food there but the drinks were certainly great. We also looked at the shops and I took Judy to the Renasance Centre. (Doesn't look right?) It was one of those holidays when you don't seem to do much, but you fall into bed at night and don't remember going to sleep. We even watched some videos. Must be a first for Gran!!

Judy is so different up at Gran's. More like she was when I first met her. I didn't feel like fighting with her and she stopped telling me what to do. Neutral ground Gran said. Judy said it is difficult coming into someone else's home like she did. She hadn't realized how much I liked looking after Dad and she had no idea I was such a good cook. If she'd known she'd have found it very useful. I nearly told her that she hadn't tried very hard to find out, but decided not to. I told her how she wasn't always fair and how Glen got away with murder and that sometimes I thought Dad loved him more than me. Whew! It was so great being able to say that. I'd said it to Gran before and she told me to talk to Judy. I never thought I would. Judy was surprised and said that Dad was always saying how great I was and that Glen thought he was the one nobody loved. It's weird what goes on in people's minds, if you ask me. She said Dad had been frantic with worry when I ran away and that

he'd even cried. That made me feel awful. I was glad
when he came up for the weekend. I'd had enough
talking by then.

I almost forgot to tell you what happened to Glen
two days ago. He got a skateboard for Christmas and
he's not that crash hot at it yet. I was just going into the
bathroom when I heard him come in. I thought he said
something so I yelled at him not to go in there as I was
going to wash my hair. He took no notice so I went up
to the bathroom to drag him out and he just fell into my
arms. I wasn't expecting it so I had to let him go and
he fell in a heap on the floor. There was blood
everywhere. I couldn't see where it was coming from at
first and then I saw he had a big gash above his right
eye. It was horrible, really gross. He started to mutter
and then he got up and was sick into the loo, luckily for
me. I didn't know what to do so I gave him a cold cloth
and got him to lie down. Then I went next door and Mrs
Ash came over to help. She was great. We took him to
Casualty at the nearest hospital. They stopped the
bleeding and said that they would stitch him up. He
had to have five stitches. I went to phone Dad and he
said he'd come right back. By the time Judy got back, it
was all over. She went up to the hospital straight away
but they wouldn't let her bring him home. She was
mega upset. He rang about half past six the next morning
and asked Judy to come and get him. They'd woken
him all during the night and shone a torch in his eyes to
see if he was okay! He looked as white as a sheet when
he got home. He'd been skateboarding down the hill to
our house and he'd hit a stone and gone over on his head.
He doesn't remember walking home or how he got to
hospital. He just remembers that I let him drop!! Dad

and Judy were glad I was home and he had someone to help him. Judy said I handled it well.

I'm off to get a film for my camera. We have to have taken some photos before next Monday. Not long before I see you. At least I can say it's this year.

Love, Brook
P.S. The fridge list has disappeared!!

Dear Madonna

I think that's what I'll call you after seeing those latest shots of you. They are so excellent. Having long hair makes you look like a film star. Whoever took them knew what they were doing, believe me. What was your photography course like? Mine was fun. We spent mega bucks on paper and film, but Dad and Judy didn't seem to mind. We had to go out on assignments and take photos of people in markets. One day we went down to the Rocks. It really teaches you to look at things. Dad took me to Flemington market and I got this great shot of masses of hub caps and another one of a gorgeous looking Italian guy selling apples. He made me taste a bit of the apple he was cutting because he said I had laughing eyes!

The studio was a bit grotty but there were all these great looking people, all dressed in black with trendy haircuts. The sort that are almost shaved at the back and then stick out in a sort of shelf. They all wear lots of dark eye shadow and have high cheekbones. I'm going to look that way, I think it would suit me. Paul does too. Paul is this great guy I met there. He's left school and is starting at Randwick tech this term. He's doing graphic design. He's an excellent artist. We used to meet in a coffee shop in Oxford Street at lunch time and he drew all these funny pictures of the people round us. It was so hard not to laugh. Then we used to walk in and out of the shops and he would tell me about the antiques and things. He's just so different. He looks Slavonic. If you don't know what that means, look it up!! His kisses make me want to melt and my legs feel all weak. Does Dan do that to you? I love being in love, it's so great. I lie in bed at night and think of him and imagine all the things we could do together. Last night I dreamed that he'd climbed in through my bedroom window. He's meeting me at Rachel's place tomorrow. I can't wait. He lives quite near us at Mum's. It's just so rad to have someone who understands what I think and feel.

Mum and John are moving to Adelaide. They told me last night. John's firm have an office there and Mum has got a job doing something at the uni. The latest she can leave is the end of this month. John has almost been crawling to me he is so scared I'll make a fuss and spoil things for him. It makes me a bit uncomfortable. It's not as if I could stop them anyway. I'll be able to go and visit them. It's good that Mum has found someone because I know she's often been miserable about Dad and Judy. Remember how you used to come and stay with me so that she wouldn't cry when I went back to Dad's? At least she doesn't do that any more. I'm off to bed, will write again soon.

Lots of love from someone who is brim-full of it,
Brook

Dear Donna

News hot off the press. Paul and I have split. What happened to your young romance I hear you ask. Well, it was romance on my side but for Paul it was . . . you've guessed it . . . sex, and that's all. Rachel, David, Paul and me all went to West Head the Sunday before last. It was hot so we decided to take one of the paths down to a deserted beach. We went for a swim and mucked about for a bit then Paul started taking photos. Somehow we ended up at the other end of the beach to the others and he finally persuaded me to take off my bikini top. He said he wanted to capture the changing texture and beauty of my soft silky skin, the light was perfect for it. Then he took some close-ups and before I could do anything he pulled my bikini bottoms down and threw me on the sand. I was really frightened and started to yell, but he put his hand over my mouth and told me to shut up. Why else had I brought him to this beach, he said. Wasn't I asking for it? It was gross. I couldn't believe this was happening to me, it was so hideous.

Luckily, Rachel had heard me yell, and she came down the beach with David to see if anything was the matter. Paul was furious and looked quite different, sort of snarly and mean. When Rachel said that I was only just fifteen, he got even madder and said that I'd been leading him on and pretending I was older than I was. He didn't have time for little flirts who were still virgins, and he stormed off up the hill. I felt so humiliated I broke down and cried. I'm not sure whether they were tears of rage or shame or shock. I felt stunned. Rachel said it was time I grew up and that if I picked up guys I knew nothing about I was bound to get into trouble. David told her not to be so rough on me, and then we walked back to the car. Except of course Paul had driven off without us. It took us ages to get home. Judy thought I looked pale and asked me was anything the matter, but I decided not to tell them. They couldn't have done anything, they didn't know about Paul, and I was still feeling awful about it. I feel much better now, and think maybe I was a bit naive. I think I'll stay away from guys for a while, tangling with them is too painful specially when I haven't got anyone I can trust to discuss them with. Famous last words!

Do you realize it's a whole year since you left? Writing like this has become part of my life. Dad was asking me what I found to write about and when I told him he laughed. He reckons you must have a distorted picture of our lives, lurching from one crisis to another. No author writes about all the days when nothing much happens, it's much more fun to write about the excitement. Anyway, you understand because it's the same with you.

Our latest excitement was Judy's car. She hates anyone else driving it but Dad persuaded her to lend it to him to take Glen to cricket because his was acting up. He rang about an hour later and asked her did she want to hear the good news or the bad news first!! The good news was that he and Glen were okay but the bad news was that he'd totalled her car! When she said, 'I could kill you,' he laughed and said that she nearly had. We went to look at the car. It was a real mess. He'd gone into the back of the car in front and then the car behind had slammed into them. They'd had to get out through the windows. Glen had a great time telling everyone about it. He could remember much more than Dad could. Judy and Dad have been having awful fights over it. I don't like it, it reminds me of how Dad and Mum used to fight before. I couldn't stand starting all over again. It's funny, isn't it? For nearly a year I've hated her, and now I'd be almost sorry if she went. She's annoyed with Dad because he has left her to do all the running around to the NRMA and the wreckers and she's getting behind with her work while Dad just goes on with his. Dad, of course, is quite oblivious to that and thinks that giving her $500 is all he needs to do. Sometimes I think men don't understand things very well. I can see what Gary meant about Judy having a hot temper.

One of the boys in our year died on the first day of term. He fell out of a tree and hit his head on the metal railing below. No one realized how bad it was at the time. It has been like a cloud over the school for the last three weeks. He was such a great guy, everybody knew him and liked him. Mr Minute, the principal, talked to the whole school on Friday and said how we should look to the future and not get stuck living in the past. The best way to honour Tim's memory is to go on into the future but go on more thoughtfully.

Yours thoughtfully,
Brook

56

Dear Donna

What is it about Paul that makes you so down on me?
Why? Why? Why? Your letter makes me sound like a
slut. I didn't 'pick him up'. It wasn't like that at all.
When Paul walked into my life it was like living in colour
instead of black and white. He appeared when I didn't
know anybody at the photography studio and he was so
understanding and made me laugh when I was down.
He listened when I told him about Mum abandoning me
and how Dad was obsessed with Judy and Glen. He
knew what I meant about having to make new friends
at school at my age and I thought he cared about me
and had taken me under his wing. He seemed so
sophisticated and I thought he really liked me. How
was I to know it was all an act? Okay, maybe I was on
the rebound from Matthew and not thinking clearly,
but that's all. Just because you've been going with Dan
for so long doesn't mean you know it all. I hate it when
you write that way.

    I also feel mad at Mum. She's gone off to Adelaide.
We spent all one week packing up her stuff, and I
realized another part of my life has gone for ever. I won't
be able to go up to Kuring-ai for the weekends. I won't be
able to get away from Glen and his spotty little mates,
there'll be nowhere to go when I have fights with Judy
and Dad. And how am I going to see Rachel and Emma?
When I grumbled to Mum, all she said was that it
wouldn't change my life, I'd still be living with Dad and
I could spend the holidays with them in Adelaide. All
she cares about is herself. She never thinks about me.

How can her job be more important than staying in Sydney near me? Why couldn't John have stayed in the Sydney office and Mum kept on with her old job? I know she liked it. Why do parents have children if they don't really care about them. There ought to be a law against it.

Then I began to think that maybe it's all my fault. If I'd spent more time with her, especially when Dad first left, then she might have been happier and she wouldn't have needed John. But I have my own life to lead, and there was Matthew, and Dad needed me too. It wasn't up to me to look after her. It's not my fault she drank so much. I'm glad she's happy, but why can't she be happy in Sydney??? Adults are so selfish, I'm not going to be like that.

Yours sincerely,
Brook

Dear Donna

This is your correspondent in Adelaide, filing her latest report. Wow! It's quite a place they've got here. A much bigger house than in Sydney. I have a room of my own that's mine even when I'm not there. It's a boring city compared with Sydney, not a lot to do and really dry and dusty. We have to spend ages each day watering the garden.

The plane trip was excellent. Really mega, mega great. Dad took me to the airport and we checked in my bag then we went and had a drink at the bar. I had a Campari soda, which was disgusting, it tasted like cough mixture, so I changed it and had a Pimms instead. Yum! I had a seat by the window so I took masses of photos as we left Sydney. I wasn't at all nervous as we took off. I was too busy looking through the things in the pocket in front of me. They brought round more drinks and I had another Pimms. I must have looked twenty at least.

After that I took out the cigarettes Debbie had given me and asked the guy next to me if he minded whether I smoked. He gave me a really funny look but said it was okay by him. Then I found I hadn't any matches. I asked the guy for a light (I could smell he was a smoker) and he asked me if I was sure I wanted to smoke so I gave this very sophisticated laugh and said that I liked a cigarette with my coffee. He gave me a lighter, not matches and I couldn't get it to work. I was

59

bending over it struggling with the bloody thing when suddenly it lit with a whoosh and set my hair alight!!!!!! It didn't actually go up in flames but sort of sizzled and there was this hideous smell of burning. The guy was really great. He picked up the lighter and cigs, which had spilled all over the place, and suggested that I waited until I got home before having my cigarette. (The poor guy must have been desperate for one himself because his mouth had a sort of twitchy look.) The stewardess came running to see what the smell was, but he just said there was no problem. I was so embarrassed. Why do these things always happen to me? I'm glad I've got some experience of flying before I make the Hong Kong trip.

Mum and John were there to meet me. When we got back to their place I discovered another girl there, the same age as me. John's daughter, Elizabeth, it turns out. They hadn't mentioned her because they weren't sure that she would be living with them and they didn't want to worry me unnecessarily!!! What a shock. The worst thing is that she's beautiful. She's tall and has red hair and a great skin. Her mother is dead and she spent last year in America, with her grandparents I think. To hear them talk you'd think she's been everywhere. Her clothes are mega-expensive looking. She goes to school in Adelaide and has already made a whole lot of friends who all come round to the house after school. It took me so long to find you and Emma, and then I moved to Gymea and nobody has given me a chance there except Debbie and Barb – she's so lucky. They are at school during the day, and Mum's at work, so it's been boring except over Easter.

Mum is just full of how great John and Elizabeth

are. She's even got her sewing machine out and has made us both a dress. I can't believe it. But somehow it doesn't feel like home. I feel more like a visitor, as though I have to ask before I go to the fridge. Do you know what I mean?? It's weird, I think I could be friends with Elizabeth. She's good fun and has asked me to go with them when they've gone out at nights. But just when I think it's okay she starts sucking up to Mum something chronic and Mum falls for it every time. So I sit there at meals feeling furious and trying not to say anything to John or Elizabeth. I just talk to Mum about how great Sydney is and how I miss her and try to make her see how great I am and how Sydney would be better for everyone. John keeps telling Elizabeth how good I am at sailing and photography and stuff, but I wish he'd shut up, he makes it worse crawling like that. He's irritating even when you know he's trying to help.

I go home tomorrow and then it's only eleven weeks until I see you. I can't wait.

Love, Brook

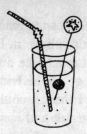

Dear Donna

Sorry I upset you by being so cranky with you in my
letter before last. I've thought heaps about Paul and why
I got sucked in so easily. I think I understand how I
needed someone just then and there he was. When I
wrote I guess I wasn't feeling as good as I pretended, so
your comments hurt. I know you'll always be there for
me, and I will be for you too. It will be so great to see
you and be able to talk instead of writing. I hope you've
warned Dan what we are like together.

You won't recognize me when you see me. I've had
my hair dyed and cut really short. It has been raining
non-stop for the last two months and I was so bored and
looked so pale and scungy that I decided to use the
money John gave me to do something mad. Deb and I
went into Sydney to this great place in Centrepoint and
chose a style out of the books there. It's mega short at
the back and sides but longer on top and sort of up in
the front. The colour is called polished mahogany. Dad
calls it henna and thinks it looks awful, but I don't care.
Everyone else likes it and I feel like the guys at the
photography school. I wear black all the time except at
school. Dad is so conservative. He doesn't realize half
the school doesn't wear uniform.

Nothing much has happened here recently, it's been
too wet. Can't even play netball. I've been grounded
for two weeks because Judy's black dress got ruined. I
borrowed it because it was perfect for a party I was

going to and Judy wasn't there to ask. I didn't think she'd mind. It got a couple of tiny cigarette burns in it and someone spilled some beer on me so I threw it into the laundry basket when I got home. Unluckily for me Dad did the washing next day and it shrank really badly because it was cashmere. How was I to know? I'm also studying hard. I'm scared that Dad might change his mind about Hong Kong if I don't get a good half-year report. We have moderators in August and I know that Judy thinks I should work all through the next break. Groan. It's slack having four parents. There's always someone who can mess things up.

Gotta do my maths homework. Write soon.

Brook

Dear Donna

I've waited and waited but no letter from you. You're
not still upset are you? I'd really freak out if I couldn't
write to you. I'm still grounded and I'm just so bored.
I really don't think I can manage much more of this. I
need to be able to get away from Judy. She can be a
real cow. Dad would never have grounded me just for
a mistake with a dumb old dress. Sometimes I think
she positively enjoys making my life difficult. I'd really
like to tell the old tart what I think of her, but I know
that if I do I won't be allowed to go to Hong Kong.

Now that Mum's in Adelaide I'm allowed to have
one long phone call a week, up to an hour. She pays one
week and Dad the other. The only trouble is that she is
often too busy to ring. And when she does, all she can
talk about is smart arse Elizabeth. I felt like spitting
chips last week when she told me the plans they were
making for Elizabeth's graduation, and this ace dress she
is going to make for her. For heaven's sake, that's
months away. Not even a mention of my graduation.
Mum also asked did I want to go ski-ing with them in
July. She makes it sound as though she wants me to
come, but she knows I'm going to Hong Kong and
nothing would keep me away. I was almost tempted for
a minute, but then I thought of Elizabeth in her fancy
American ski gear, swishing down the slopes like an
expert, hanging on to Mum's every word and making
it with the ski instructors when Mum had gone to bed.

I could just see myself being pushed into the background like a discarded Barbie doll, sent off to the beginners' class while the others did the exciting runs. Then in the evening I'd have to sit at dinner listening to their adventures, smiling until my face felt it would crack, and all the time I'd be boiling inside with a mixture of pain and rage. I decided it wasn't going to be much fun, so I said no. Mum just said I could make up my own mind.

I have a reason for being so fed up about being grounded. You'll die when you hear it ... are you holding your breath? Yes, it's a guy!!!! Again! Two weeks ago I met this really spunky guy at roller-skating. I've been going to the rink on Friday nights. It's a good place to meet people and I've got quite good at roller-skating. I noticed Nathan as soon as I walked in. He's dark haired, of course, good looking and an excellent body. Tall and slim, with a tiny bum and long legs. He's also the best skater there, I found out from Debbie. He goes in for competitions and has heaps of gold medals. He knows Deb and came over to talk to us. He's in year eleven at one of the Caringbah schools. At the end of the evening he asked me for my phone number. The others couldn't believe it, they've been trying to catch him for ages, and I didn't do anything at all but just be there. We went to the movies later in the week. I can't remember much of the movie because we sat in the back row and had a great time. He's a fast worker, quite different from Matt. Nathan has great hands, they are slim, brown, gentle and strong. I just loved what he was doing, it could have gone on for ever. He's got some friends who all live together in an old house and they have heaps of parties. We went there last week and it was so great. I'm scared legless that he will find someone else while I'm grounded. He has been ringing me up most days though. I didn't tell you about him before because I thought you'd think I was a nuthead. He likes my hair, thinks it's sophisticated!!!

Write soon. I'm missing your letters,
love from Brook

Dear, Dear Donna

Was I pleased to get your letter! I thought something
must be wrong when you didn't write, but I would never
have thought of a bus accident. It would have been
hideous if you had been badly hurt. Lucky Dan's father
is a surgeon or you all might have had to wait ages
before you got help. What happened to the teacher who
was driving? How long will Dan be in plaster for? That
will cramp your style a bit!!!

I'm having an excellent time with Nathan. He's full
of energy and ideas. I've never met anyone like him
before. He hardly ever sleeps at home. His parents don't
seem to mind him spending nights at Jason's old house
and he can do pretty much what he likes. He can even
go home at five in the morning if he wants to. He's got
a job working as a chef's assistant on Thursday and
Friday nights. He gets mega bucks for it so he's always
taking me out, or we go with the guys from the house.
He took Friday last week off specially for me because
we wanted to go roller-skating and then on to a surprise
birthday party. Guess what . . . Judy wouldn't let me
out because I had only done thirteen days of being
grounded and it was for two weeks! Can you believe
that anyone could be so mean?? Dad and she
disappeared into the bedroom and I yelled and
slammed my door I was so frustrated. Dad then came
and told me that I really had to abide by the rules, and
dear Judy added that if I didn't like the way the house

was run I could always go to live in Adelaide and that, anyhow, she was getting sick of my attitude. I was so furious I couldn't eat any dinner and just stayed in my room. Sulking, so Judy said. What a bitch. To think I almost liked her at one stage.

When I told Nathan he asked me whether my bedroom was on the ground floor and I said yes. (He's never been to our house.) He told me to calm down at home to make it look as though I'd accepted Judy's rules and that when they'd all gone to bed he'd come and get me and I could get out of the window. I was a bit nervous at first, but then I remembered that Dad never comes into my room without knocking and there would be no reason for him to come in after I'd gone to bed anyway. I was so helpful for the rest of the week I'm surprised I didn't explode. I heard Judy telling Dad that I just needed a firm hand and I'd be fine, that he was too soft with me and that he was afraid I wouldn't love him if he was strict with me. Adults have such stupid ideas. As if I would ever stop loving Dad, even though he's done some pretty dumb things.

On Friday it all went okay. I went into my room after dinner and said I wanted to do some study and that I was going to bed early so that I could have a rage on Saturday night to celebrate not being grounded any more. Judy and Dad watched TV and at about eleven-thirty I heard Nathan outside and off we went. The party was so excellent. It was at one of those really big houses near the water. They must be really rich. There was an enormous pool, all floodlit and a covered area with a bar that was almost as big as our house. (Not the bar, you nut, the room.) We all sat around and got drunk as skunks. After a while I felt gross so I went outside with

Nathan and chucked up in the gutter. God, I felt awful.
I thought I'd die. I don't remember getting home.
Nathan says he and two mates took me home and had
a hideous time getting me through the window because
I kept going all floppy. They were scared Dad would
hear them. I couldn't get up the next morning, even Judy
thought I looked ill, so I spent most of the day asleep.

I hate being at home at the weekends, there's nothing
to do and I just lie around feeling spooked. Often I lie
in bed with Razoo purring on my chest and nibbling my
chin and wonder whether Mum ever really loved me. I
think of the way she took off to Adelaide and how
sucked in she is by Elizabeth. Then my mind seems to
explode and I hate her and I know why Gary thought
Judy was a bitch. Then the next minute I want John
and Elizabeth to die in a horrific car smash so that Mum
will be sorry and need me to go and look after her.
Then it will be just her and me again, like it used to be,
and she'll have to come back to Sydney. Sometimes I
think I'm going crazy. What do you think? I can't even
tell Emma about it. I couldn't take the way she'd look
at me. I'd feel really dumb. It's much easier writing it
down. Then I wonder what it will be like when I see
you again???!!!

Yours Wondering,
Brook

Dear Donna

I bet you're sweating it out over exams and wishing you'd done more revision. Going to Hong Kong means you'll be a whole year ahead of me when you come back. If you ever do! Tell Dan that I'm beginning to believe in Fate, all the people I need are miles away from me and I can't do a bloody thing about it. Dad's right here but he might as well be miles away and Mum is still doing everything she can to make that poser Elizabeth like her. Hey, don't jump to conclusions, I'm still going with Nathan.

Last week we went to another party, this time at Jason's house. I told Dad that I was going to spend the night at Deb's, and I really did mean to. Deb, Craig, Nathan and me all went to the disco up at the hotel. It was excellent but the drinks were mega expensive so we didn't get to the legless stage. Nathan drove us back to the old house in Jason's Torana. What a buzz! We went 140k down the road before the freeway. It was unreal. We were laughing so much and shouting at the other cars as we went by. Nathan almost side swiped one old retard, you should have seen her swerve. We had to pick up some more friends, we were so squashed in that we could hardly breathe. I stuck my legs out of the car and some slack cop saw me and pulled us over. I got fined $30. Nathan was just under the limit, which must have been the miracle of the year. He can play a didgeridoo and he says that means they can't catch him with the breathalyser. The party was great. You should see the mess those guys live in. We all got so spaced out that we slept on the floor at Jason's and didn't wake up till twelve.

I think Judy suspects something, she's much more observant than Dad. She's always on my back and won't leave me alone. She even follows me into my room and keeps talking at me. When I tell her my point of view Dad gets cranky and says stupid things like, You're just like your mother. Now Judy's nagging me over my stereo set. She says she's fed up with me playing Heavy Metal full blast. They are never satisfied. If I'm in my room I'm in a black mood, if I go out I'm never at home. Why do they think I want to be at home when it's perfectly obvious that Judy hates me and is trying to ruin my life. I think she'd like to kick me out. She nearly cracked up last time Gary came to stay because she found him in my room at one o'clock in the morning. Adults are obsessed with sex. All we were doing was talking, although I actually think he's an ace guy. He thinks a lot and has interesting ideas about things.

If you are wondering why I'm writing to you today, it's because it's school excursion day, so Nathan and I went to a movie and I'm writing this in a coffee shop while he is at the doctors. I feel like a real correspondent writing my despatches to HK. I'm going to do work experience with either the *Herald* or the local paper in September. Here he comes, only one more letter before I see you. I can't wait.

Love, love, love,
Brook

Dear Donna

I don't know where to begin, all hell has broken loose here. I'm not even sure I'll be coming to Hong Kong. Last week Dad and Judy said I couldn't go to Debbie's because they'd been told she'd been caught nicking things from Coles and she'd been put on a bond, whatever that means. They are so judgemental. Everyone does dumb things sometimes, she just happened to get caught. If it was okay to stay with her before, why not now? She needs support, not isolation. Anyway, that meant I had to leave by the window to meet Nathan and the others at the disco. I left a note to say I'd gone shopping with Deb, in case they looked in the next morning. Just my luck, Glen got sick during the night and was throwing up everywhere, so Judy stuck her nose into my room to see if I was awake. She went bananas when she found my bed empty and the note. They rang all my friends' olds at two in the morning and then called the police. Dad was out in the car driving round like a maniac, and all the time I was at Jason's place. When I walked back in on Saturday afternoon, all hell broke loose. It was all so unexpected that I couldn't think quickly enough and I copped the lot.

Dad was as white as a sheet and his eyes looked as though they were in dark holes. He didn't say much, but just kept sucking in his breath through his teeth. Judy went off her head. She yelled and screamed and said she was sick of putting up with me and my moods, that she'd tried everything and that I was an ungrateful little wretch. Nothing she did was good enough. I was rude and unpleasant to live with and I was destroying her life with Dad and she wasn't going to let me. I was just looking out at the water creeping up across the mud and watching the pelicans catching fish, letting Judy's tirade wash over me, when I heard her say that I was a slut, all I could think about was sex and that she knew for a fact that I'd been with guys at Jason's house, why else would I go there so deceitfully. That was it, I'd had enough. No help from Dad, still standing mute in the kitchen. So I walked into my room, got the rest of my money and walked to the door. Judy tried to stop me but I was icy calm and told her that I didn't want to talk to either of them right now, that I was going to Debbie's and that when they'd calmed down they could ring Debbie's mum and come round there, then I left. I felt absolutely numb till I got to Deb's and then I started shaking all over. I couldn't stop, it was weird. Deb's mum was great, she didn't ask a single question. She came over, put her arms round me and stroked my hair and before I knew it I was bawling like a baby. Don, you should have seen me. I was sobbing and hiccupping and went on and on. Deb's mum's shirt was soaked by the time I'd finished. Then she left me with Deb and phoned Dad and said to come around the next day, she'd look after me until then. My whole body felt sort of drained.

Deb's mum is great, really cool, and easy to talk to. We talked about Mum and how much I miss her. I even told her about Elizabeth and how Mum cares more about her than me. And how my mind goes mad sometimes so I can't stop it and then I do these stupid things. She said that Mum moving so far away means it's difficult to be as close to her as before. Often that happens when kids go off inter-state to work or to uni but it's too early at fifteen. I still need her and I'm grieving for her. That felt about right, I'd never thought of it like that before. It made me cry some more. She asked me if I'd talked to Dad about all this, but I said I couldn't because of Judy. Talking to Judy about Mum feels like betraying her somehow and doing to her what she's doing to me with Elizabeth. Oh Don, life's so complicated. I've got this huge cauldron of emotions bubbling away inside me and I never know what's going to burst out next. There must be some way of keeping the lid on it. Deb's mum says turning down the heat is better!

I slept in Deb's room that night. We were going to talk some more but Deb says I gave a grunt and was asleep. Dad and Judy came and picked me up the next morning. It was a bit of an anti-climax really. We all felt wiped out. They said they had no idea that I had felt so unhappy or that I was so miserable about Mum. I'll tell you the rest when I see you, if I do, because I want to tell you something more important.

After all this Nathan and I caught the ferry to Bundeena. We took a back pack with food and a rug and went off along the cliffs, it was one of those perfect days, blue, blue sky, cold in the breeze but warm out of it. Nathan made me tell him everything that had happened. When I'd finished his face was soft like I'd never seen it before and his brown eyes had tears in them. He put his hands either side of my face and very gently kissed me on the mouth. It was so sweet that I actually felt my heart flip over inside my chest. We lay down then and went on talking and kissing until one particular kiss made me feel I belonged together with

Nathan and that we were the two halves of a whole. There were no barriers between us at all. It was like looking into a deep well and not being frightened of what you'd see or of being seen. We said things I couldn't even say to you, Don, and I felt as if all the creases of my life were being smoothed out. Then we lay there, half sleeping, half talking. I stroked the soft downy hairs on Nathan's chest and buried my face in his armpits, loving the smell of him. The sun went down and it got cold so we went back to the ferry. It felt so great walking hand in hand. Then I thought how it was only yesterday that Judy had called me a slut. That made me laugh because we had made our own decision about what was right for us and it was nothing to do with what Judy had been talking about. Donna, is that what it is like for you? Why didn't you tell me?

Dad says he'll be phoning your olds in the next few days. Hold your thumbs.

Love & trepidation,
.Brook

STOP PRESS! STOP PRESS! FAMOUS WAR CORRESPONDENT BROOK CAMERON ARRIVES HONG KONG FRIDAY JULY 1ST EVENING CATHAY PACIFIC STOP DON DAN TO MEET STOP ROLL OUT RED CARPET STOP LETTER FOLLOWS STOP

Donna, Donna, Donna

Can you believe it??? I have a grin from ear to ear. I
don't know what to do with myself. I can't wait for next
Friday. Dad says this will get to you after I arrive, but
I don't care. I have to write or I'll go crazy. It's like
an addiction.

Mum came over to Sydney on her own last weekend
and we had a really great time. We spent Friday and
Saturday up at Kuring-ai with some friends of hers. They
were ace people. Emma and Rachel came to stay too.
We had a wild time. I haven't seen Mum laugh like that
for ages. Emma is an excellent mimic and had us all in
stitches doing take-offs of Kylie Minogue and Michael
Jackson. It was so great. Then, on Sunday, Mum and
me moved into this mega swanky hotel and got all
dressed up for dinner. Forgot to say she bought me a
black outfit from Oxford Street. One of those shops that
smell of incense, where Paul and me used to go. It was
an excellent evening. We were sharing a room and we
lay in bed and talked for ages. She told me how Elizabeth
had missed her mother, who died, and how she'd wanted
to stay with her grandparents but John was desperate to
have her with him. So Mum was doing all she could
to make it as easy as possible for her. It's strange that
they don't tell you that at the time, but let you go through
hell before you find out. I didn't say that though, in
case I broke the mood. Mum said that she had been so
happy that she hadn't thought that I might be jealous

or anything like that. And guess what!! I discovered that it was *Judy* who had rung her up and told her how upset I was. But it was Mum's idea to come over. We are going to do it again, but not as expensively next time. That way I don't always have to be with John and Elizabeth. It's different with Glen because he's there all the time and I forget about him.

It's been heaps better at home too. Judy said she was sorry she'd yelled at me and that in future when things bothered her she'd discuss them with me early on instead of letting them build up. She said she didn't want to be my mother as I already had one, but she could be a friend. She said she doesn't know much about bringing up girls as she only has boys and that she'll need to learn from me. She's going to give me some money to get her a camera in Hong Kong and says that the clothes there are mega cheap and really excellent. She reckons I'll be able to get a whole lot of outfits, including ski-gear. Hope she's right, it'd be great to surprise Elizabeth!! I'm glad I've got all that money saved up. Judy also said that it's not so much what happens to you that matters, but what goes on in your head and how you think about it. It really makes a difference. I know what she means. I already feel better about Mum and Elizabeth now I know what Mum is trying to do.

In case you think I have done nothing but talk in the last week, I should tell you I've seen quite a bit of Nathan. Mostly at the skating rink. He's training for the speed trials and is hoping to get a place on the NSW team. It was so funny the other night. We'd been watching videos at Debbie's place and at about eleven we decided to go to Nathan's house because he said his olds had gone out to some ball or other and wouldn't be back till really late. The lights were on because his brother was watching TV in their parents' room. He stuck his head in to say goodnight and I heard this female voice say, Hello, Nathan, you're in early, who's your friend? I nearly died. It was his mother!!! Nathan was real cool and said that he was walking me home and we'd stopped in for a drink, and told them who I was. His father sounded a bit surprised and said he hadn't realized we lived so close. I felt a real twit and my face went all red. I couldn't get out fast enough. I don't know what they must have thought.

You probably won't believe this, but I don't think I really want a sexual relationship with anyone yet. I know what happened two weeks ago gave me a mega buzz, and I really love Nathan, but when I think about going all the way, I'm not sure. So many of the guys just use their girls and then drop them and everyone gets hurt, or they want you to spend all your time with them and I don't want to give up all my other friends, like Deb and Barb, Emma and Rachel. And I'm scared legless about getting pregnant and all the rest. How much do guys of seventeen and eighteen know about AIDS and do they care? Lots of them act as though they are immortal! I don't want to find I'm HIV positive or have some smelly little baby ruining my life. I want to be a journalist first. Whew! Now I've written it, it will be easier to talk about.

I'm getting almost spooked about seeing you after all this time and all these letters. Writing them and sending them off is not the same as saying things face to face. Do you think I'm crazy?! Deb asked me if you were Chinese yesterday, she thought you must be if you live in Hong Kong!!! I told her your Dad and mine grew up together in England but that you're a real dinkie die Aussie, born in Wollongong for God's sake. Don, Don, Donna. I can't wait to see you. Don't be late at the airport, will you???

See you THIS WEEK, by the time you get this.

Brook

Dear Don and Dan

I almost think of you as one person now. I miss you so
much I ache all over. Barb and Deb are good fun but I
can't talk to them like I can to you. They got such a buzz
from the black Reeboks. Debbie is wearing hers with
black tights and a mega tiny black mini-skirt and a
jeans jacket, she looks rad, specially with her long hair.
We all went over to her place and tried on all my gear.
I'm going to stun Elizabeth. Am I ever!!! Yuk, I can't
believe I'm back in this cold weather with all the
teachers nagging at us about the lousy moderators next
month. It's all they can talk about.

The reason I'm feeling so down is that Nathan's
family are all leaving for London in a few days. His
father has been posted to be bureau chief or something.
I asked him why he had to go, he could always live
with us or with Jason in his house with all the other guys,
but he said his Dad thought it would be a good
opportunity for him and it would give him a new start.
I think he really wants to go because it sounds exciting,
but he says he's fought it every inch of the way. He
hasn't got enough money to live here and finish school.
I don't mind as much as I would have done if I hadn't
spent the last few weeks with you. I got quite a few things
straight in my head. It's hard to explain, but it's as if
Nathan's gone sort of shadowy. I still love him but I think
I love the idea of him better than him. And there isn't
that hollow feeling inside me anymore. I don't need

him so much. He says I've got harder, but I feel more as if I know where I'm going and it's not the right time to be in that sort of deep relationship. I need to be free. I'm not ready to be part of a pair that does everything together. It's different for you and Dan, you've got something fantastic between you, but that's not what I want for me. So one minute I'm feeling pikey and the next minute relieved and excited. What a nutcase!!

I've been lying on my bed listening to my Chinese tapes and dreaming of all the things we did in Hong Kong. Razoo has been lying on my chest purring his head off, he's so pleased to have me back. He keeps putting out his tongue and licking my nose. He follows me round like a dog, or races ahead of me if he thinks I'm going to the kitchen. I keep remembering that fab day we water skied all the way to Cheung Chow behind Simon's boat. It felt like flying. And how wrecked I was when we stopped. My legs wobbling like jellied eels. And that mad Ben who took his motorbike to bits in his father's flat while he was away and how we sprayed the place with aerosols to get rid of the smell. What happened to him? Now he is a spunky guy, even wants to travel, like I do. No good thinking that way, I guess.

Got to go and do some homework. I've got a whole heap of catching up to do. Will write soon when I have some more energy.

Miss you lots,
Brook

Dear Donna

Well, that's one more lot of tests over. They weren't too bad. In fact they were quite easy. Perhaps old Lingo and his pals will let up on us for a bit. It makes me sick to think of you and Dan still sailing and water skiing every day with no school. Typhoon Rhonda made a real mess of Hong Kong, I saw it on the TV news. What happened to Ben's father's boat? Tai Tam looked like a boat junk yard, didn't he keep it in Tai Tam? And what about that old European engineer who lived on the old junk by the pier? I bet he took his boat out to sea to ride it out. I wish I'd been there to see the water crashing over onto Connaught Road.

Judy's been at it again, but this time it turned out okay. She and Dad think it's about time I did something 'humanitarian' instead of gym, netball, surfing, you name it. So . . . they put my name down for the Australian Theatre for Young People!!! I nearly died when they told me. Anyway, I went along just to see, feeling scared almost legless, but what a buzz! I've never seen so many brilliantly spunky guys in one place and some of them are around twenty! They were rehearsing for a freaky play they'd written themselves, something to do with a twenty-first century post-Holocaust. Sounded hideously morbid. I didn't have to have an audition. I just go along every Wednesday

evening to this place in the Rocks. I've been twice
so far, it's rad. We play what they call theatre games.
That means they tell you to improvize a situation
round a quarrel, or something sad, and then you go
off in pairs to work out what you're going to do. Sort
of bringing it to life. I've got heaps of ideas about
angry and sad situations after everything that's
happened at home in the last year, that's for sure! The
teacher told me I had a good feel for dialogue!! What
a surprise!!!

One of the guys in our class is in year eleven at our
school. He's called Andrew. We go into the Rocks by
train together. (Perhaps Judy is more cunning than I
thought!) He's more the athletic type than an actor,
with fair hair, a wide mouth and a fantastic wit. He has
me falling about with laughter on the train. Nothing is
safe from him. No, I'm not falling for him, he's just a
friend. Remember, 'I still haven't found what I'm looking
for'? That's still the way I feel. It's weird the way songs
say things for you.

Nathan left on Thursday. I feel sort of spooked
without him, but it wasn't as deadly as I expected saying
goodbye to him. You could see him beginning to think
ahead to England and what he was going to do there
and that I was already part of his past. Although I had
made up my mind that I didn't want that sort of
relationship right now, I still miss him. There's a sort
of empty space. Judy said that you always have a special
feeling for your first lover. I wonder if she knows how
close we were? Sometimes it's easier to talk to her than
to Dad about things like that. Maybe because we are

**both women. And you know how old-fashioned
Dad is!**

Still missing you to talk & laugh with,
Love,
   Brook

Dear Don-and-Dan

Thanks for your excellent letter. The typhoon damage
sounds hideous. It's hard to believe that the school
roof could go after surviving eighty years. Lucky
most of the new building is finished. What a nerd Ben
was to be driving down Magazine Gap road when
all the nullahs were like waterfalls. He was lucky he
didn't get killed as well as writing off his father's car.
Guess what! I got a letter from Ben! I told you he
had the hots for me! Do you still play squash with him
Dan?

I've been having an excellent time with Andrew. Last
weekend we went up to that fabulous fish restaurant
on the beach with some friends of Dad's. It turns out
that Judy and Andrew's mother were at school together.
I knew there was some smart-arse idea behind drama
school! Andrew just laughs and says his mother is like
that too, and he grabs whatever opportunities come his
way. He can't understand why I won't have sex with
him and has even talked to his father about it. His Dad
told him to see it as a challenge!!! I like his Dad, he
goes to work on this mega fantastic motorbike. Andrew
isn't hassling me, I'd give him up if he did. Anyway, we
were on the harbour bridge on the way home and we
stopped the car. I got out and was looking under the
bonnet, poking around in the engine while Andrew was
yelling and screaming at me as if I was the one who
knew what to do. People kept slowing down and giving

us funny looks. Then we saw the breakdown truck's lights, so I hopped back in the car and we took off in a hurry, laughing ourselves silly. And I thought Andrew couldn't act!

Dad and I have got our picture in one of the glossy mags, called Mode. Even Dad had to admit I look excellent with my dark hair and black leather jacket. I'll send you a copy. We went to a tie Auction where they were auctioneering all these ties and autographs of famous people. I got a Dick Francis tie for you two, as I know you like his books. Dad got a metal elephant that had been part of George Bush's presidential campaign, it's the Republican symbol, in case you didn't know. Afterwards someone came up and offered Dad $200 for it, and he only paid $10! He didn't part with it though, as he wanted it for a friend. So did it cost $10 or $200? We have all been arguing about it.

Answer in the next edition!

Drama school is still a buzz. We have to work on something we can show to our parents and other people at the end of term, so some of us are going in on Sundays to work on it. We are trying to decide between something really emotional so that we can show off a bit, and something minimal and trendy. Will let you know. Maybe we could do both.

Next week I'm on work experience, so no school. I can't wait. I'm going to work on the *Sutherland Times*, our local paper. I wanted to go to Dubbo, but Dad said I was too young and it was too far. Why are parents so protective? They seem to think we don't know anything. Debbie is going to work in a hospital, her father said hairdressing would be better!!!! Barb is going to a stockbrokers, she wants to be a yuppie!!! She dragged me off to see *Wall Street*, an excellent movie, but I think she may get a shock.

Write again soon, love + all that,
Brook

Deeeaar Dooonnna

I'm so exhausted I can hardly move. What a week it's
been. Working on a newspaper is just ace. The editor
and sub-editor were both really cool. The editor looked
just like TV. Ruffled hair, wrinkly, untidy, and a cig
hanging on his bottom lip. The sub-editor was the one
I had to report to. I wasn't allowed to do all the things
a cub reporter would do because the editor said I was too
young. But I did get to go with one of the reporters to
interview a woman of twenty-two who had knocked
down two little kids getting off a bus. It was really
hideous. All she could do was cry. How could she live
with herself? She'd had two schooners and there was a
cop sitting by her bed. I didn't see the mother.

Sitting in on police interviews was interesting. The
cops are often really tough, but not like the movies.
Lots of it was mega boring. When there was nothing else
for me to do, in other words if they thought I had time
for a cup of coffee, they sent me down to the morgue to
get skulls!!! That's what they call the head shots or
photos of important people that are kept in huge files in
case they are needed in a hurry. I just loved it, even
though I'm tired. Everyone was fantastic to me and want
me back in November. I'm still not smoking, although
my clothes all stink of it.

Drama workshop ends on the twenty-fourth and then
I'm going to Adelaide to see Mum. I have to audition
for a play the ATYP is putting on in November before

I go, but I'll tell you more about that next time. I'm going to veg out tomorrow, if Andrew hasn't got some hare-brained scheme planned. Debbie and Barb had a good time too. There's more to being a yuppie than meets the eye!

Yours with closing eyes,
Brook

Dear Donna

This may be one of the last letters you get from me before Christmas! No, I haven't cracked up, I've just got a part in the production ATYP is putting on at the end of November, and that means rehearsals start in ten days, theatre practice two evenings a week and all of Sundays. And there's that little matter of year ten exams at the beginning of November and another week with the *Sutherland Times*. Dad and Judy are beginning to wonder what they've started! I don't have time to get into hassles with them anymore.

This theatre practice has been excellent. When I do anything that taps into some of my feelings about Mum, Dad and Judy I can be really expressive, and then when we've done the improvisation, it's as though the feelings have faded into the shadows. At first I was scared they'd gone for good and I could only act them out once, but it's not like that at all. Do you remember when I told you about being like a cauldron? Now it's just simmering nicely and when I take the lid off it's fine, everything I need is there. Do you understand what I mean? The other thing that's so cool is that I feel much more grown-up and in charge of my life. I don't know where that comes from. I know that Mum and Dad and Judy still bug me, but I can tell myself that they are doing their best for me, but they don't know as much about me as they think they do, and I don't want them to either. It's not being sneaky, just having my own life. Barb is beginning to feel like this too, and Rachel and Emma. I still see them sometimes. Debbie is still fighting, but her dad is so stupid.

The play we are doing is *Spring Rising* written ages ago by some Danish guy with an impossible name. It's about young people growing up in old-time mega-inhibited Denmark. One of the boys knows all about sex and explains it to another one using drawings. The school finds the drawings and he is sent to reform school!!!!! One of the girls gets pregnant and dies because her mother is ashamed of her and frightened of her second husband who calls in the local abortionist, who kills her. The husband doesn't care because she's not his daughter anyway. (So much for me feeling that I have it tough!! At least my olds aren't archaic.) The second boy commits suicide because he doesn't know how to talk to girls! It sounds like a bunch of nutcases cracking up, very morbid. But it's not. There's hardly any scenery and we do a lot of dancing around in white floaty scarves. Sort of symbolic.

I got the part of Elsbieta, one of the four girls. I don't have to say much but I'm on stage quite a bit. The audition almost scared me legless. We did it in pairs and had about two weeks to practise it. I had to be Wanda (that's the one that dies) asking her mum to tell her about how babies are made. (If you don't know that now when you're fourteen they'd give you heaps!) A lot of stuff about storks, which Wanda knows isn't true. I did it with Jackie, who is nearly twenty. She's been part of ATYP for ages, she's excellent and a great actress. She got the main part. We had to do it on the stage with all these people sitting in the stalls making notes on us and whispering. If you go on long enough you forget about them. It's just so cool to get a part. I keep thinking I'll wake up and it won't be real, not first time round.

Will write and tell you more next time, gotta go and pack. Adelaide tomorrow. I feel wrecked.

Love to you both,
Brook

Dear Don

Did you get my photos? What did you think of Liz? I can't wait to hear your reaction. She's not so much of a poser as she used to be, quite human in fact. They were all on holiday so Mum took Liz, Renate (her best friend) and me ballooning. Mum didn't actually come with us, she took us and picked us up. It was so great. The pilot has some control, but not as much as in a plane. Something Liz had never done before. It was mega cold so I wore my ski gear and looked excellent. Everybody said so. Judy thought I was dumb to take it!!!

Mum looked pretty good too. I think the newness of Liz has worn off a bit, she even forgot to pick her up from gym one day, and no, it wasn't anything to do with me! Liz doesn't suck up so much. John is the same lame-brain as ever. He's so super good it's sick. I think he's frightened of me in a sort of way. But who cares? He's never done anything for me, so why should I like him? Liz isn't a bit like him. I went with her and Renate to one of the best hotels in Adelaide (not as fabulous as Hong Kong) and we had a real rage in the bar. Then these creepheads we'd been eyeing up began to get real heavy, trying to look down our T-shirts, undressing us with their eyes and making us feel naked. We didn't know how to get out without them following us. Renate suddenly said in a loud voice, 'There's Dad!' but I couldn't see her father anywhere. She gave me a shove and then all three of us walked out behind this old guy trying to look as though we belonged to him. We must have done an ace job, because the guys didn't follow us even though we were nearly dying of laughter. As soon as we got outside we split our sides and the old man gave us such a look.

I only spent a week in Adelaide because I had to get back for theatre practice. Mum actually took a week off and came back to Sydney with me and we both went to stay with her friends near Kuring-ai again, which was excellent. I had plenty of time to catch up with Rachel and Emma while Mum yakked with her friends. We all went with Mum to the kite festival at Bondi. There were heaps of Malaysians there with these fabulous Chinese-looking kites. Some of them spoke Cantonese, I recognized it. Afterwards we all went to the gelato bar and made pigs of ourselves. Mum is much better without John. She came along to theatre practice one evening, just to see where it was and what we were doing.

Practice nights are Wednesday and Friday. We started by reading the play right through and talking about it and getting people's ideas about how it should be. It's not the sort of place where you get told what to do, it's more co-operative. Andrew didn't get chosen, which is a real pain, although I'm not surprised. There's one super spunky guy called Jake who's about twenty. He left school two years ago. I'm not sure whether he works or is at uni or tech. He's got a great voice and is an experienced actor, it's obvious. But he's not a show-off at all. I hope Dad doesn't freak out when he finds out more about this play!!! It was all Judy's idea in the first place!

While I was up at Kuring-ai, Razoo got run over. I still can't write without crying. Gary rang me on Saturday to say that Razoo had had a bit of an accident the day before. He'd been knocked down by some gross driver who just left him by the side of the road to die, he hadn't even stopped. Razoo dragged himself up the neighbour's driveway and they'd found him in their gutter and got Gary. Gary said he was a real mess, too badly hurt even to fight them. Cats often bite when they are hurt. I rang the vet and he said he thought Razoo would be okay, cats mend really well. I asked could I come over and see him, but he said better wait until the next day, after they had operated on him. He was sure he'd make it through the night. So I raced home early from Sunday theatre practice and was just phoning the vet when Gary came in and said, 'Razoo's dead.' It was hideous, I burst into tears and Gary hopped over the counter and wrapped his arms round me and I just howled and howled. Poor Razoo, I know he would have wanted to see me, I was his favourite person. And I wanted to say goodbye and hear his purr once more, because cats can purr right up to dying. I felt so angry with that lousy vet I could have rung him up there and then and told him what I thought of him. There'll never be a cat like Razoo, he was really a supernova spunky animal. Dill is also miserable without him and is yowling round the house like a banshee, which irritates Judy. Bad-tempered old tart.

Must stop writing and go to bed. Year-ten assessments in two weeks and everyone's on my back again, Mum, Dad, and Judy. I miss having Razoo trying to sit under my desk lamp when I'm working and keep remembering the times I yelled at him and threw him off my desk.

Love, Brook

Dear Donna

I told you I wouldn't be writing much, hope you don't
mind. I'll fill you in on what's been happening. I'm
wrecked, it's my first free evening for weeks. First of
all, thanks for the Johnny Diesel album. I just love that
track, 'Don't need love,' it says it all. You always were
excellent at choosing something to hit the spot. I had a
rad birthday. Dad and Judy took a whole group of us
to the Centrepoint Tower restaurant, where we could
choose from the buffet and eat as much as we wanted.
That way Rachel and Emma could come, as well as Barb
and Debbie and two of the cast from ATYP. The waiter
brought out this cake with a sparkler on top, the band
played Happy Birthday, everyone clapped and looked
at me, and I nearly died of embarrassment. Mum sent
me $50, a real bonus. The trouble with all this
rehearsing is that there's no time to earn any money.
Not much time to spend it, either! I half thought Judy
might not let me go out so close to the exams, but Dad
said it would do us all good to spend Saturday night
off, and Glen was off somewhere with his mates, so that
was okay.

The exams weren't too bad. We had a whole week
of them, but we were allowed to stay home and revise.
I think I've done okay. Don't know how well Deb has
done, she was crying after the Maths test. She's got so
much potential but she wastes half of it fighting her dad.
He's such a jerk. He needs kneecapping. School is a

joke from now on, no one really cares if we're there or not. Hard to get Dad and Judy to appreciate that!!

I went back to the *Sutherland Times* for the second work experience. It was great to be back. This time I was allowed to sit in the ops room and go out with the reporters to interviews after accidents and domestics and things like that. The editor said I wasn't to go to anything violent, but you can't always tell what it's going to be like!! I had my name on one piece. I'll send you a copy. The editor said that I should let him know when I was ready to apply for a cadetship on a paper. Cool, eh?

It was gross trying to fit in theatre practice and work experience. I was so wrecked that I took the day off school yesterday, and not a murmur of protest from Judy. I just lay around in my room watching soaps and listening to sad songs on my tape deck. I was missing Razoo too, he's usually curled up on my stomach when I feel that way. I've got his bowl on my shelf and won't let them use it for Dill.

Theatre practice is fantastic. The pace is hotting up, we have our costumes and the play is taking shape before our eyes. After rehearsal we all go out together and have lunch in one of the places in the Rocks. Usually we go Italian because it's cheap and the guys say they need more than just sandwiches. When you are spending two evenings and all day Sunday together you develop very close relationships with everyone. It's having a common interest and working as a team that does it. Just standing quietly together waiting to go on stage, with butterflies in your stomach, and knowing the others feel the same way. I can't describe how exciting it is. The noise and bustle of getting the set together, the smell of greasepaint in the room where we all change, the lighting and sound effects team trying out different things, but mostly it's making something come alive that before was just words on a page, and knowing that we will be out there doing it. They say the tension is the worst before the first night. I can't wait. Wish you could be there. One day you'll be here to see a production, that's for sure.

Andrew is doing another workshop, so I see him sometimes. I think he's a bit spooked at not having a part in our play. He's gone Gothic, dyed his hair black and changed how he dresses. It's all old and black, except for his white shirt hanging out the back. And he has this huge cross he wears, and . . . wait for it . . . he never goes out without putting on eye-liner and making his face up! So he looks like he's crawled out from under a stone and has these dark intense eyes. It's really rad.

Donna Aitkin, you are the worst ratbag in the whole universe, a real smart alec aren't you???!!!! Why didn't you tell me??!! How could you be so secretive?? And not give even the smallest clue??!! Dad just came in to say he had a big surprise for me and when I looked big question marks at him he said that he thought someone I was very close to had a ticket for 28 November, our first night. I thought he meant Mum, but he strung me along a bit and then told me it was you!!!!! And that you are all coming back to Sydney for good just before Christmas and that you will be staying with us until your mum and dad get back. Super fantastic!! I can't believe it, is it true??? It's the best thing that's happened all year. It's so rad! So this is really my last letter, I'll be meeting you at the airport at 6 am on Saturday next week. But Don, I'd forgotten, what are you going to do about Dan? I know he won't be with you on Saturday.

What a lousy way to have to test out your relationship. You haven't split have you? Dad didn't say anything about it, so I hope not. I'll bring heaps of Kleenex to mop up tears of joy and sorrow and be there for you like you've been there for me.

Signing off with love + mixed feelings,
Brook

THE DIVORCE EXPRESS
by Paula Danziger
Piper £2.99

Divorced Parents can act worse than their Kids!

You'd have thought that, after the divorce, Phoebe's father would have been more understanding about Rocky. Away from her mother, best friend and boyfriend, Rocky the racoon seemed to be the only friend Phoebe had. And so what if he kept knocking over the garbage?

It's funny how one week everything seems miserable and the next, everything's good. Just as Rocky was facing a death sentence, her father changed his mind. And then on the bus Phoebe met Rosie, who quickly became her best friend. From then on, the future seemed a whole lot brighter . . .

GIRLTALK
- all the stuff your sister never told you
by Carol Weston
Pan £5.99

A new edition of the best selling book for girls. It gives you the lowdown on life, and the update on:
BODY - looking and feeling your best
FRIENDSHIP - you don't like everybody, why should everybody like you?
LOVE - what you should know before saying yes
DRUGS, ETC - the facts without the lectures
FAMILY - can't live with 'em, can't live without 'em
MONEY - the buck starts here
EDUCATION - getting through school, and after . . .

USEFUL ADDRESSES

The National Stepfamily Association
72 Willesden Lane
London
NW6 7TA
UK
Office tel: 071 372 0844
Counselling service: 071 372 0846

The Stepfamily Association of Victoria
PO Box 551
Blackburn
Victoria 3130
Australia

Stepfamily Association of N S W Inc
10 Short Street
Thornleigh
New South Wales 2120
Australia
Contact tel: 02 484 3788

These organisations provide support, advice and
information for all members of stepfamilies and
those who work with them.